NOT FROM THE STARS (HIS MAJESTY'S THEATRE BOOK 1)

Christina Britton Conroy

For Cindy—
If you like this:
Book 1,
I'll send the rest of the
series— All Best—
Christina B Conroy
6/19/23

First published by Endeavour Press Ltd in 2017.
This edition published by Lume Books in 2020.

Table of Contents

Forward

When I was a child, my parents bought an antique music box that played sixteen-inch brass disks. My favorite was:

HENRY VIII

Morris Dance

This tune so haunted me, I made up stories, humming it as background music. Years later, I learned it was Edward German's incidental music, composed for Lyceum Theatre's production of Henry VIII, in 1892. A few years later, that music was used at Her Majesty's Theatre.

When I first wrote a story about a Victorian schoolgirl escaping a forced marriage to become an actress, I did not want to upset readers with historical mistakes. I chose a late year, 1903, and a fictional London theatre, HIS Majesty's. I was told no one taught acting in 1903, still, I imagined a top floor rehearsal hall and an actor-manager who taught acting classes. I also chose a play for the theatre to produce in early 1904, *The Tempest.*

Soon after finishing my first draft, I was on holiday in London. I buried myself in the London Theatre Museum Library and the Westminster Reference Library. I read a 1903 play list for a real HIS Majesty's Theatre, and nearly hyperventilated. A delightful librarian explained that the theatre's name changes with the gender of the monarch, and Edward VI became king in 1901. Many of my inventions turned out to be historically correct.

The theatre's founder, actor-manager Herbert Beerbohm Tree, taught acting classes which developed into the Royal Academy of Dramatic Art.

His one new production in 1904 was The Tempest.

I telephoned Her Majesty's Theatre, and a kind stage-manager gave me a backstage tour, including the beautiful top floor rehearsal hall.

I read that Herbert Beerbohm Tree was very generous leasing, and even lending his theatre to charities and other theatre companies. My novel is set while his company was actually away, touring America.

Huge thanks go to the London Theatre Museum, Westminster Reference Library, The Old Bailey Reference Library, Wildy & Sons Books, and especially Michael Kilgarreff and the Henry Irving Society.

Special thanks to Betty Anne Crawford at Books Crossing Boarders, and my agents Donna Eastman and Gloria Koehler at Parkeast Literary.

Sonnet XIV
Not from the stars do I my judgement pluck;
And yet methinks I have Astronomy,
But not to tell of good or evil luck,
Of plagues, of dearths, or seasons' quality;
Nor can I fortune to brief minutes tell,
Pointing to each his thunder, rain and wind,
Or say with princes if it shall go well
By oft predict that I in heaven find:
But from thine eyes my knowledge I derive,
And, constant stars, in them I read such art
As truth and beauty shall together thrive,
If from thyself, to store thou wouldst convert;
Or else of thee this I prognosticate:
Thy end is truth's and beauty's doom and date.

Chapter One

Yorkshire, England: December 23, 1885

Emily reached the landing as a scream exploded from the bedroom. She lurched back, crying.

A large elderly woman, sleeves rolled up, hands and apron covered with blood, wiped sweat off her face with the back of her hand. Blood smeared across her forehead. "Where in 'ell are those towels?" she shouted down the curving staircase.

"Cummin' Mrs. Graves," the maid called, stumbling up the stairs.

"How much longer!" demanded a smartly dressed, dark-haired young man from the floor below.

Mrs. Graves scowled at him over the carved banister. "T' doctor's doin' 'is best, Mr. Roundtree. Ah said y' should 'ave fetched 'im yestiday." She roughly took the pristine white towels. "Gi'- me - them 'ere then." She started back into the room. There was another scream.

Anthony Roundtree stamped his foot. "Just see that she doesn't die!"

Another scream made him look up and shudder.

"I'm here, sir." Trembling with fright, breathing heavily, the Anglican priest hurried in, wiping beads of perspiration from his face. "They sent me to pray with a dying woman." He looked around wide eyed, mouth open, awed by the opulent furnishings. He flashed a weak smile. "Thank you for trusting me."

Roundtree curled his lip, started up the stairs, and caught his foot in a carpet tear. "Damn it! Everything in this bloody house needs repair." He shouted back to the priest, "You've got a wedding to do first. Hurry up, Vicar!"

The priest stumbled after him. "But, this is most irregular. Shouldn't I pray with the poor unfortunate...?"

"The poor unfortunate's the bride, and she's not dead yet. Hurry man, or we may be too late." A scream sent them running double time.

"I was told this was a married woman."

"My brother's widow. Hurry, damn you!"

The priest entered the room and sunk to his knees. In front of him, in an ornately carved bed, lay Bertha Roundtree, chalk-white, her face contorted in agony. Her legs wide apart, she screamed as the doctor forced a metal instrument inside her. Blood spurted like a fountain, covering the doctor and soaking the fine embroidered bed linen. An old woman, dressed in somber black, clutched Bertha's hand, and rocked back and forth, quietly crying.

The priest pressed his hand over his mouth to keep from vomiting.

Roundtree pulled him to his feet, bellowing, "The marriage certificate, damn you!"

The priest dropped his briefcase, spilling papers in a random pile on the floor.

Roundtree's quick eye found the appropriate form. He seized it, strode to a polished corner desk, dipped a silver pen into a crystal inkwell, and held the paper over Bertha. "Here, sign this!"

Bertha lurched violently, and the old woman let go of her hand. She stared at the paper. "*Was ist das?*"

Roundtree shook the pen and paper. A blotch of ink spilled on Bertha's face. He grabbed her hand, forced the pen into it, and held it to the paper. Writhing in pain, Bertha wildly marked the paper and dropped the pen. Quickly retrieving it, he pointed it at the priest. His voice dropped to an ominous whisper. "Sign this, vicar."

The priest, white-faced and shaking, took the pen. "This is highly irregular. A wedding may only be performed on sacred ground."

"There's an old chapel behind the house, that's close enough. Your buggering my stable boy was highly irregular. Sign, or I'll tell the bishop and your wife."

Doctor Vickers gave a mighty heave with his metal forceps. Bertha screamed, and the priest dropped the pen, spurting ink across her abdomen. Roundtree seized the pen and stuck it back in the priest's hand, holding it steady while he signed the certificate.

"The pronouncement, Father Folen. Say the bloody words!"

The priest mumbled unintelligibly and crossed himself. "Anthony Roundtree, do you take...? Sorry, what's the lady's name?"

"Bertha -- yes I do, and so does she." Roundtree checked the paper and smiled. As he read down the page, his smile disappeared. "Mrs. Graves, come witness this, quickly."

She stood still. "I'll never, sir…,"

"You'll sign it, or your son will go to prison for the money he owes me."

"Tha' wouldn't do that, sir."

Bertha's eyes were closing.

"Now! Damn you, woman! Sign!"

Mrs. Graves let out a sob. She signed the blood and ink stained document.

Doctor Vickers pulled a scalpel from his bag. "The mother's gone, the child may yet survive." He sliced Bertha open. The only sound was the weeping of the older women.

Father Folen sat against the wall, focused on nothing. Anthony Roundtree bent down, hissing into his face, "Do your final prayers now, man, before the bitch goes to hell."

The priest staggered to his feet. "In the Name of the Father, and of the Son…,"

Suddenly, piercing through the sobs of the women, the cry of a newborn child filled the air. Mrs. Graves held up her hands. "Praise be to God!"

"What is it?" Roundtree demanded.

The doctor, covered in blood and sweat, handed the child to Mrs. Graves. "You have a daughter, sir."

"Yes, yes! This is perfect." Roundtree kissed the marriage certificate and sped from the room.

Chapter Two

London, September 1889

"Jerry, thank heaven!" Tommy Quinn screamed with joy and raced at full speed. His hard leather heels clattered over uneven cobbles as he rushed toward Jeremy O'Connell. From a distance, Jeremy's tall slender frame, sleek brown hair, pale skin, and large brown eyes looked stunningly beautiful. The day before, the twenty-five-year-old actor had accepted a tour with famous actor-manager Henry Irving. Tommy was heartbroken and threatened to kill himself. Now, he hurled himself into Jeremy's arms.

Horrified, Jeremy pushed him away. "Not in the street, silly fool. We'll be arrested." Guiltily looking in all directions and seeing no one, Jeremy sighed with relief and smiled at his adorable companion. Tommy Quinn was twenty-four. His short, athletic body, large gray eyes, thick brown hair, and mischievous smile, were set off by one crooked tooth.

Jeremy shrugged. "Irving's offer is very tempting. The money is good and the roles first-rate. The problem is, he recreates old productions. I could be forced to parrot his last actor, and not allowed an original thought. I am better off staying here."

"You've got *Henry The Fifth*."

"Oh yes, Mr. Tyler used Hal as a bribe. He is making me play cloying Claudio as penance."

Unable to resist Tommy's sweet eyes, Jeremy gave him a playful hug, glanced over his shoulder, and saw a terrifying flash of navy-blue. A uniformed Bobby marched towards them, swinging his nightstick. They sprang apart. The Bobby winked an eye and swaggered by.

Jeremy shuddered. "That was too close."

They walked a block to Henry Street, through the stage-door of the Strand Theatre and downstairs to the rehearsal room. The worn floorboards were grimy. An ancient coal stove, and dozens of actors puffing acrid cigarettes, clouded the air and yellowed the walls.

Fred, the grizzled stage-manager, sat behind his rickety desk, squinting through scratched spectacles. He pushed a sign-in sheet and pen towards Jeremy. "Heard you might be eloping with Henry Irving."

Jeremy sent Fred a twisted smile and scribbled his name. He grimaced at a pile of cloth-bound script, took one for each play, sat in a rickety chair, and tentatively opened *Much Ado About Nothing*.

"Mr. O'Connell? I'm Katherine Stewart, playing Hero."

Jeremy glanced up at sparkling china-blue eyes, a pert nose, and rosebud lips framed by long, honey-blond hair.

"You're a wonderful actor. I saw you on tour in *The Bachelor's Dilemma*." Her cheeks flushed with excitement.

Jeremy flinched. "You saw that piece of fluff? Well, I am glad you enjoyed it." He stood and offered his hand. "How-do-you-do?"

She reached her hand and an armload of scripts clattered to the floor. "Oh, dear! Dancers are the world's clumsiest people."

Jeremy helped collect her scripts and noticed that her figure was slim and shapely.

Her excited words rushed out. "This is my first engagement, as an actress, that is. I've never spoken lines, but I've been on stage since I was a baby." Embarrassed, she lowered her eyes. "It was Variety and Review, I'm afraid. A family dance act. They're vexed with me for leaving. I have to send money home to make up."

"Mr. Tyler is paying you enough to send money home?"

She nodded happily. "A guinea a week."

"And for that princely sum, I suppose you are providing your own costumes?"

"Not for Hero… but for the supernumeraries." She smiled hopefully, "…and I'm covering four principals."

Jeremy shook his head in disgust, as Fred carried over a small table. "Take a seat, everyone. Mr. Tyler just arrived."

All the actors scrambled, scraping chairs into a slapdash semicircle. David Tyler entered the room. Fred handed him the sign-in sheet.

Katherine sat motionless watching Tyler's every move. He was a striking, elderly gentleman, with an almost military bearing. His well-tailored suit hung perfectly. Since he was no longer an actor wearing makeup and false beards, he had grown elegant sideburns that blended with his thick gray hair. The only men in London without facial hair were actors.

Tyler addressed the company. "Good morning ladies and gentlemen. I trust you have met our newcomers... Miss Stewart?" Katherine stood, smiled sweetly, and sat down. "Mr. Killen?" A good-looking young man stood, smiled, and sat. "We shall read through *Much Ado'* this morning and put it on its feet this afternoon."

Shakespeare's play is marvelous, but the rehearsal hall was stifling. The moment they were dismissed Jeremy snatched Tommy outside.

Katherine followed with her arms full of scripts. She squinted against the bright sunlight, then stopped when a young man carrying a large suitcase sped toward her. Jeremy recognized his old friend, actor Simon Camden--a delightful surprise.

Simon was brash, funny, blond, and beautiful. Jeremy's very first season, Simon had played Mercutio to his Romeo. Formally a ballet dancer, Simon's body was sinewy, supple, and very strong. They had shared dressing-rooms on the tour. Even seeing Simon in layers of traveling clothes, Jeremy remembered the adorably soft blond curly hairs sprinkling his arms and chest. They darkened slightly below his belly and around his well-endowed organ. Much to Jeremy's disappointment, Simon had had no interest in sharing that with him. That fantastic piece was gifted only to ladies, and it was gifted constantly.

Simon dashed toward pretty Katherine Stewart barking, "Kathy, Kathy, I auditioned for Henry Irving's tour and he engaged me on the spot. Good thing I hadn't unpacked."

Katherine's pretty mouth dropped open. "B'But, you just returned last night. You said you were going to find an engagement in London, that we would stay together."

He shrugged it off. "Darling, you've got an engagement and lodgings, you'll be fine."

"But, that boarding house is horrible."

"We've lived in worse places."

"We were with my family. I've never stayed anywhere alone."

"I'm sorry, darling, I'll miss my train."

"Then miss your sodding train!"

He dropped his suitcase and flung his arms around her. "Darling, when I get back, marry me. Then we'll be together for...,"

"Marry you?" Stiff and fragile as a wounded doe, she clutched her scripts and hurried down the road.

Simon called after her, "Kathy…" She vanished around a corner.

He shrugged, hurried a few steps, collided with Tommy and Jeremy, and laughed. "My God, it's a poufs' convention."

Jeremy forced a scowl. "Bloody hell, Simon. Watch where you're going."

"Listen you lot, I'm touring with Henry Irving: The Master. Can you believe it?"

Tommy and Jeremy exchanged knowing looks.

"I'm late for my train." He hurried off, then hurried back. "Jerry, you can save my life."

"I'm not sure I want to." Jeremy bit the inside of his cheek to keep from laughing.

"Katherine Stewart--you saw her just now--she was at rehearsal. You must have met her."

Jeremy chuckled. "Oh, yes, the delicious new ingénue. What about her?"

"She's *my* Kathy. My dancing partner, when I was in Variety."

"*That* girl is the 'Kathy' you have written letters to, all these years?"

"Yes."

"The girl you *say* you are going to marry?"

"Yes."

"Good grief!"

Simon swung a pocket-watch into his hand and checked the time. "I promised to stay with her, but this tour… with Irving."

"So, what do you want from me?"

"Take care of her for me." Tommy burst out laughing and Simon glowered. "Not like that, you slag." Simon jammed the watch back into his pocket. "Look Jerry, you always mother-hen the new chaps."

"Yes, the new *chaps*." Tommy bent double, laughing.

Simon ignored him. "Please Jerry. For me. For old-time's-sake."

Jeremy shrugged. "Well… I'll do what I can for her."

"Thanks. You're a real toff." Simon heaved his suitcase into both arms and dashed from sight.

Tommy wiped tears from his eyes. "Dear God. At least we know who took the tour in your place."

"Simon Bloody Camden. I didn't even know he was back in town."
"He's not. He's gone again."

Chapter Three

Jeremy hated playing Claudio in *Much Ado About Nothing*. He thought the character was dull and stupid. Rehearsals were agonizingly boring. He counted the hours until the show would open and he could concentrate on his next role. Katherine played Hero, in love with Jeremy's Claudio. Every time Jeremy even glanced at Katherine, she stared back with huge, beautiful eyes. He hoped she was studying his acting, and cringed thinking she might be falling in love. She knew he and Tommy were lovers, but she watched his every move and blushed whenever they spoke. He kept his promise to Simon and gently encouraged her.

The Strand Theatre Company rehearsed three plays at once. *Much Ado'* opened first. *A Midsummer Night's Dream* opened second, with Tommy playing Oberon. *Henry V*, Jeremy's leading role, opened last.

One morning, Tyler rehearsed the women's scenes. He interrupted Katherine's speech with, "Louder, Miss Stewart!"

She looked startled, then screeched,"...*of this matter*
Is little cupid's crafty arrow made,
That only wounds by hearsay...."

"Enough. Let's break for lunch." He threw down his script. "Miss Stewart, do something with your voice." He marched from the room and Katherine looked stunned.

The actors stretched, chatted, and started leaving. Almost at the door, Jeremy remembered his promise to Simon and walked back to her. "Need some help?"

"What's wrong with my voice?"

"Sounds like a fishwife. It's your breathing. It's all wrong."

"My breathing?"

"Your whole posture. Before every entrance, you go up on your toes. It looks very strange."

She gasped. "But, people always told me I look beautiful. I always do that, it gives me..." She gracefully balanced on the balls of her feet, and lifted her arms like a ballerina ready to leap on stage.

"You are not dancing now, so stop it. Just walk naturally."

"Oh." She lowered her arms and stood like a stick. "How should I breathe? I never thought about it."

"You're breathing too high. You have to relax your stomach, let the breath push your voice out."

"Push out my stomach? I couldn't."

"Then you will never breathe properly." He turned on his heel and started out. Tommy followed.

Katherine scampered after them. "I'll do it. Please show me how."

Tommy grimaced and checked the clock. "Come on, Jerry. We've only got an hour."

Equally miffed, Jeremy seized Katherine's hand, held it against his stomach, and inhaled. She looked amazed by how much his stomach expanded. As he exhaled, his stomach pulled in, releasing a wonderfully resonant: "Ahhhhh…" He dropped her hand. "I'm hungry. Let's go to lunch." The men were almost at the door, before Jeremy looked back. Katherine had not moved. "You're not eating?"

"No."

"Saving tuppence to send home?"

She flushed a flattering pink. "I'll stay and practice breathing."

Jeremy muttered to Tommy, "She's adorable. How could Simon just leave her here? He is such a slag." They fled up the stairs

Katherine was a quick study. Watching the older actresses, she learned to breathe while cinched into a tight corset. Her voice lowered and resonated nicely.

One morning, she glided downstairs, expecting an uncomplicated rehearsal as Puck's Fairy in *A Midsummer Night's Dream*.

As she signed in, Fred whispered, "Nancy Ellison's down with croup. Yer rehearsing Titania."

Katherine dropped the pen, whispering frantically, "But I don't know the role, not all of it. Will Mr. Tyler let me use the script?"

He wiped ink off her hand. "He won't like it. Better try without. Just do yer best, love."

Minutes later she faced Tommy as Oberon. He took stage, crooning seductively:

"I do but beg a little changeling boy

16

To be my henchman."

She clenched her hands together and looked into his large gray eyes.

"Set your heart at rest:
The fairy land buys not the child of me.
His mother was a…"

Her mind went blank and her eyes grew huge.
"Votress!" Fred's voice boomed.
Katherine swallowed.

"…votress of my order:
And, in the spiced Indian air, by night…"

"Full hath!" Fred's voice again.
Katherine blinked hard. "Full hath…"
Tyler slammed his hand on the table. "Miss Stewart, this is intolerable!"
She was nearly in tears. "I'm sorry, Mr. Tyler. I've been learning the other roles. I never expected Miss Ellison…"
"We never expect anyone to become ill, but they do. That is why we engage understudies. Skip ahead… Oberon: *'Well, go thy way.'*"
Rehearsal ended at dusk. When Tommy and Jeremy rushed from the stage-door, Katherine was waiting for them. "I'm so sorry, Mr. Quinn. I ruined your rehearsal. Is Mr. Tyler going to sack me?"
Jeremy whispered, "No, he will not sack you, but you must do better."
Tears filled her eyes, and Tommy impatiently patted her shoulder. "Just go home and study. You'll do fine. Come on, Jerry." He turned to go and Jeremy pulled him aside.
"Tommy, love, I have to help her. She will drown if she doesn't get some direction."
"Why do *you* have to help her?"
"I promised Simon."
"To hell with sodding Simon."
Jeremy chuckled, affectionately pinching his leg. "Go home to the cuddlies. Give Neil a kiss for me and I'll see you both tomorrow."

Tommy scowled as Jeremy seized Katherine's arm and led her down the street. She gazed up like a grateful child.

Jeremy was not particularly hungry, but guessed that Katherine was famished. They stopped into a grocer's for bread, cheese, cold meats, apples, and wine, then walked a few streets to his small block-of-flats.

"Wait here a minute." He passed her the grocer's bag. "If my landlord is home, I shall have to sneak you up the back stairs." Katherine gasped as he loped up the front stairs, two-at-a-time. In a moment he was back, smiling. "It's all right. He's gone."

He retrieved the bag and led her through an ornately carved door paneled with cut glass, into a darkly wallpapered hallway. She followed him up a flight of stairs. Wall sconces flickered with faint blue gaslight.

As Jeremy unlocked the door to his flat, he saw Katherine's eyes lower. Her shoulders tensed. He guessed she had never been alone, inside a man's bedroom, and felt she was doing something immoral. Once inside, he closed the door and hung their coats on brass hooks in the wall.

She looked around, shyly smiling. "This is beautiful."

"Thank you. I would never use that adjective, but it is certainly comfortable."

The L-shaped room contained a large bed, wardrobe, desk and chair, all made from the same dark wood, carved with designs of grapes and plums. A dark-green spread covered the bed, and matching curtains hung on two large windows. Small rugs covered most of the wide uneven floorboards. Rows of books stood on neat shelves. Everything was clean and tidy. One small corner was the kitchen nook. Jeremy took plates and glasses from cupboards.

"Do you prefer wine or tea?"

She laughed uneasily. "I'd better take tea. I would love some wine, but it would probably put me to sleep."

Jeremy chuckled, lighting the stove. "Tea for now, and wine later. How's that?"

"Lovely, thanks." She automatically took charge of the food.

After supper, he easily coached her through Hero. The role was simple: a young girl, in love, who thinks everyone else should be in love. She looked at him and spoke Hero's tender words. They both knew she was not acting.

18

Helping her understand Titania was much harder. After another hour's coaching, Jeremy sprawled exhausted across the bed. "Of course they are angry with each other, but why?"

Desperate to please him, Katherine's body was tense as a rubber band. "I don't know why they're angry. They both had other lovers. That makes them even, doesn't it?"

Jeremy sat up, amazed. "You're a very modern woman. So, what does Oberon want?"

"The boy."

"Good. What does Titania want?"

"The boy."

"No!" He threw up his hands. "She wants to punish Oberon. He has hurt her. That is why she went to Theseus."

She caught her breath. "Then, it's about wanting his love and fearing she can never win it." When he sighed with relief, she smiled and paced. "You are entirely correct. I was memorizing words when I should have been studying the characters and their *wants*. Oh, thank you, Mr. O'Connell." She rushed to the bed and hugged him hard. He stiffened and she backed away. "I'm so sorry, I...,"

"No worries." He forced a laugh. "I've been calling you, Kathy, all this while. Don't you think you should call me Jerry? Kathy doesn't actually suit you. You are more of a Kate. Yes, Katie, I think." She was startled, but pleased. He took her coat from the hook. "You did first-class work tonight. Now, you need a rest."

"I don't know how I can ever thank you, Mr.... Jerry. I know you're helping me because Simon asked you to, but...,"

"Actually, I had forgotten about Simon. Coaching you has been a pleasure." He helped her into her coat, then took his own.

"You don't need to see me home."

"Of course I do. Since my landlord has come home, I must take you down the back stairs, into the alley. It is not pretty.

A week later, Jeremy held a long-stemmed white rose and walked past the entrance to the Strand Theatre. Patrons queued at the box office. A placard read:

STRAND THEATRE MUCH ADO ABOUT NOTHING
OPENING TONIGHT

Within blocks of the Strand, Londoners chose between legitimate theatres, opera houses, concert halls, music halls, saloons, and brothels, providing any sort of entertainment they could possibly want. Jeremy was surprised anyone would buy tickets for their small production.

He signed in at the stage-entrance and the stage-doorkeeper handed him a letter. "Good luck, Mr. O'Connell."

Jeremy scowled. "Thanks loads. I'll need it to pull off a role this boring." He spotted the letter's return address and chuckled with anticipation.

Simon Camden
Theatre Royal
Manchester

He trotted up the stairs, remembered the rose in his hand, and climbed an extra flight to the small dressing-room Katherine shared with three other actresses. He placed the rose, with a note, on her dressing table.

To Katie,
  Break a leg!
Jerry

Three-and-a-half hours later, the make-believe conflicts were resolved. Benedick commanded, "...*Strike up pipers!*" Dancers skipped around the happy couples. As rehearsed, Jeremy took Katherine in his arms and kissed her. She clung to him and seemed startled when the curtain fell and he sprang away, to line up for the bows.

For the next several hours, cast and crew, their friends and families, stayed at the theatre, eating, drinking, and waiting for their reviews. Tommy, Jeremy, and their friend Neil lounged on one side of the greenroom. Katherine huddled in a lonely corner.

One by one, messengers arrived with newspapers, still damp from the presses. Actor-manager David Tyler opened each broadsheet, nervously reading the words aloud. The first two reviews were favorable, the third, wildly enthusiastic. Katherine sat up when they heard:

"...The evening's best surprise was Katherine Stewart's Hero. Not only has this young lady beauty and poise, but an unaffected vulnerability, sure to make every man in the audience fall in love. Miss Stewart may prove to be the new find of the season."

The entire room cheered and applauded. Jeremy was ecstatic. "Hurrah for Katie! This calls for a celebration." He hurried to her corner. "You look gloomy as a funeral guest. Whatever is the matter? You should be thrilled."

"I am, really." She tried to smile, started to cry, and fled the room. He was close behind as she collapsed in the stairwell. "Oh Jerry, I've got to get back on the circuit. My father sent a letter. They're in terrible trouble. They're losing engagements. They're starving." Tears streamed down her cheeks.

He was shocked. "But... you told me your sister's dancing the solo."

"Mary can't dance. Oh, she could, if she put her mind to it. I had Simon's wonderful choreography and we loved to rehearse. Mary's dancing partner's a lazy sod."

"You've been sending them money."

"Not enough. Simon just sent another fiver."

"Then, they're all right for a while?"

She shrugged. "For a while."

"Please, Katie, don't despair. Let me furnish you some money, just to tide them over."

"I couldn't possibly accept...,"

"After these reviews, you are sure to obtain a proper engagement next season, with a proper wage. Then you will be able to take care of them, and pay me back, with interest, if you like. You are such a lovely talent."

Thrilled by the compliment and desperate to believe him, she smiled and wiped her eyes. "Do you really think I'll get...?"

"Come along, starlet. This is your special night. We should celebrate." He held out his hand. She took a tentative step, then rushed into his arms. He hugged her tight. When they broke apart, she clasped his hand. He led her back toward the greenroom, gently pulling his hand away.

Chapter Four

October 1889

One Wednesday afternoon, a month later, Jeremy signed-in for the matinee and Fred the stage-manager pulled him aside. "I found Kathy sleeping on the floor of 'er dressing-room. She's wiv Tyler, and he's steamin'."

"Damn! I knew she needed money, but never thought she'd do something brainless." He rushed to David Tyler's office. The door was open and he saw Katherine perched tensely on the edge of a chair.

Tyler paced like an aggravated schoolmaster. "Bloody hell! This is a theatre, not a boarding house."

Jeremy hurried in. "What's all this, then?"

"She has been sleeping in her dressing room and she won't promise to stop."

Katherine was near tears. "I'm not hurting anything. I never lit a candle."

Jeremy stood between them. "Not to worry, Mr. Tyler. She will not sleep here again. We will find her a place to reside." He grabbed her arm and hauled her out.

That evening, Katherine and Jeremy sat in a teashop, sipping sweet, milky tea. He shook his head. "I knew you had left the boarding house, but I never guessed you would actually…," he shook his head and put a finger over his lips. "I feel responsible for this. I pressed you to stay."

"Oh, for goodness sake, Jerry, it's not your fault." She sighed, sorrowfully. "Nancy's offered to let me 'ghost.'"

"*You* sleeping on *Nancy's* floor?" He shuddered with horror. "No, I do not think so." A crooked smile twisted his lips. "Well, Katie dear, it appears the only alternative is, at least for the present, that you cohabit with me."

Her teacup slipped, then leveled an instant before brown liquid slopped down her front. "But, how could I?"

"I will just need to convince the landlord that we are married." A twinkle came into his eye as he enjoyed a private joke. "Do you remember the last scene in *The Bachelor's Dilemma*? I signed a marriage license. A-half-dozen counterfeit certificates were left after we closed, and I took them as souvenirs. If we sign our names, the deed will unofficially be done."

Her hands trembled as she returned the cup to its saucer. "But, it's your home. What about your... your privacy?"

He fluttered a hand. "Not to worry. Ages ago, I begged Tommy to move in with me. He refused. He prefers the house with Neil, and the other cuddlies, on Haymarket. I spend half my nights there, as it is."

An hour later, they were back in Jeremy's flat. He sat at his desk, studying a sheet of paper. Very slowly, he wrote careful letters.

Katherine unpacked her battered suitcase, and carried her second frock to the wardrobe. She hung the frock next to Jeremy's suit jacket and lovingly ran her fingers down the sleeve. He noticed the gesture, thinking it was sweetly pathetic. She watched as he concentrated, bending over his desk.

"You could have been a wonderful dancer, Jerry. You move like a panther: lean, and sleek, and elegant." Afraid she wanted to hug him, he concentrated harder. She returned to her unpacking. "Jerry?"

"Hmm?"

"You said I should send my whole guinea home, but...,"

"Do it. I am hardly a wealthy man, but I have funds enough to keep us both. Let us say that I am investing in a future star."

"I do so want to make you proud of me. And I'll help wherever I can. I'm a good housekeeper. I'll do all the shopping and the washing up, and I can mend anything. My last pair of dancing tights was more mend-than-mesh, but no one could tell."

"I am sure you will be invaluable. Come here a minute. I need you to sign this." He leaned back so she had a clear view of the counterfeit marriage license.

At first glance, it appeared genuine. She read aloud, "*On this third day of December, in the year of our Lord eighteen-hundred-and-eighty...,*" she squinted. "I can't read the year."

He nodded. "Good."

"Oh." She read further, "...*at Christ Church, Bitby.*" She thought for a moment. "Where is Bitby?"

"That is where I lived in *The Bachelor's...*,"

"...*Dilemma.* How could I have forgotten?" She chuckled and read further. "...*Service presided over by the Reverend Henry Plantagenet? Witnessed by Sir John Falstaff and Robin Hood?*"

"The property master had a sense of humor. Just sign here."

Still chuckling, she carefully signed her name.

He studied the document. "I'll catch my landlord tonight, when it is dark and he doesn't have his spectacles. He'll have a quick look, then I'll bury this."

Still chuckling, Katherine returned to her suitcase and unpacked her nightdress. She looked at the one large bed and froze like a pillar of salt. Blushing like a beet, she rolled the nightdress into a ball. "I've been sleeping on the floor. I'm very used to it. I wouldn't mind at all, if you preferred to...,"

"I didn't bring you here just to put you back on the floor. The bed is plenty large enough for us both. You needn't worry that I will try to molest you." He folded the marriage license, and raised an eyebrow. "I am rather worried that you will molest me."

Eyes bulging and cheeks burning, she sped to the bed and tucked her nightdress under a pillow. "I've only been with one man--just Simon-- and that was only to keep him in the act."

He burst out laughing. "You slept with him to keep him in the act?"

"He stayed an entire year longer."

"How old were you?"

"Oh, I was of age: sixteen. I'm almost twenty, now."

Her story was hilarious, but he choked back a laugh. "I'm famished. Let us get a bite."

"I hate your paying for everything." She started toward the kitchen corner. "At least let me fix something."

"There is no food in the flat. We can go to the shops tomorrow. Come along." He held out his hand.

She stepped to take it, then flung her arms around him. He stood stiff as granite, and she quickly let go. "I'm sorry. I'm just so grateful." She stood back, breathing hard. "I know you're only doing this for Simon, but he never expected...,"

"I am not doing it for Simon, silly twit. I am doing it for you. You are a very special talent and I will not let the world lose a potentially brilliant actress, because she cannot pay the rent."

She smiled, then closed her suitcase and pushed it under the bed.

He watched thoughtfully. "Katie love, I think we can be very cozy together, you and I, as long as you do not expect me to be another Simon."

She gasped "I don't. I promise. Growing up as I did, I have always known men who partnered with other men."

"Good. I trust you mean that. Just, don't fall in love with me. I will break your heart." She stared at the floor and he felt miserable. She was already in love with him. He seized their coats. "Come along, I'm hungry."

They ate a quiet supper at the corner pub. After a few false starts, they found themselves speaking comfortably. Jeremy never talked about his family and Katherine guessed it was a painful topic. He loved hearing her family history, with Simon Camden. He had never seen her as relaxed and happy, remembering the hard times and good times they all shared, dancing on the Variety circuit.

They were both exhausted when they returned to the flat. Behind the house were two toilets, but no other private space. Neither of them spoke their fears of sharing the bed, but Katherine seized her nightdress from under the pillow and sneaked into the dark kitchen corner. The second her back was turned, Jeremy dived into a nightshirt, leapt into bed, pulled the covers high, and pretended to read a book. Katherine returned, covered from neck to ankle in faded pink flannel. Her golden hair fell around her face, and she looked like a child. Smiling anxiously, she scurried into the empty side of the bed, pulled the covers high, and hovered on the edge of the mattress.

He said, "Good night. Sleep well."

She forced a whisper. "Thank you. Good night."

He blew out his candle and the room went dark. The dull beam from a street lamp slipped through the curtains. He could see her lying stiff as a pillar. He rolled onto his side, so his back faced her. He waited -- nothing -- she didn't move.

He spoke as kindly as possible. "If you dangle on a precipice, you are liable to fall off."

"I'm fine." She still did not move.

Without thinking, he reached his arms around her, and drew her into the center of the bed. "There. Now we can both get some sleep." He kissed her forehead.

"Thanks, I- I'm so grateful…"

"You have thanked me enough. Now, go - to - sleep." He gave her a cuddle, snuggled his back against her front, and lay still. She kissed his ear. It tickled and he chuckled. Finally, she snuggled against him and closed her eyes.

Chapter Five

Very quickly, the fake Mr. and Mrs. Jeremy O'Connell became comfortable roommates. They had an identical sense of humor and got along really well. Katherine borrowed a wedding ring from wardrobe and wore it with silly pride.

Both actors and stagehands were flabbergasted. Unmarried theatre people often invented lies so they could live together, but no one expected it of the gorgeous, flamboyant Jeremy O'Connell. Most of the women and some of the men were blatantly jealous.

Tommy Quinn hauled Jeremy into their dressing room and slammed the door. "Bloody Hell, Jerry! Where are we going to go? Is that sniveling *girl* going to stay away all night so we can have privacy?"

Jeremy whispered through a clenched jaw, "That 'sniveling girl' has more courage than the lot of us Nancy Boys. I begged you to live with me, but you refused. You wanted to be near Neil and the other cuddlies. You've got a whole house. You know I'll come to you."

"Maybe I won't want you to come to me." Tommy pouted like a spoiled child. "Maybe I'll invite Archibald Perry instead. He's been dying to get into my knickers."

"That slimy slag?" Jeremy laughed. "That aging fop is dying to get into *my* knickers, and thinks you're the back door. I only tolerate the pompous ass because he writes me good reviews. His daily tabloid crap isn't worth…,"

"Archie has a huge following."

"Yes, of frustrated shop girls and lonely spinsters."

"They buy a lot of papers."

"Bloody hell, Tommy! Nothing needs alter between us."

"But, the house is a shambles."

"The house would be magnificent, if you lot would just tidy it."

"Damn you, Jerry! You're nothing but a buggering piece of slime. You…" Screaming like a banshee, Tommy lashed out with every foul word in his vocabulary. If Jeremy didn't silence him, someone would break down the door. He jammed Tommy against the wall, kissed him, and rubbed him, hard. Tommy's screams shrunk to soft moans.

Jeremy pushed away. "Damn it, Tommy. You're behaving like a lunatic and turning me into one, as well." Tommy's crooked tooth had jabbed Jeremy's lip. He checked his reflection in the mirror. "Good, there's no blood."

The call-boy's strained soprano rang through the door. "'alf 'hour, gents."

"Thanks Danny." Jeremy sat at his dressing table, and started to make-up.

Tommy sniffled, "I love you, Jerry. I can't help it."

"Shh," he whispered, "I love you too, silly sod."

Tommy pouted. "Why can't I borrow a wedding ring and pretend I'm your…,"

Jeremy laughed sadly, "Do shut up, and get ready for the play."

*

Katherine and Jeremy made a strikingly handsome couple. Jeremy towered over nearly everyone as he gracefully wove along busy walkways. Katherine, fair and lithe, looked absolutely stunning, walking on his arm. The tilted brim of her hat rested just under his chin, allowing them to pose effortlessly, and enjoy the admiration of other pedestrians. Everyday visits to shops, exhibits, parks, and walks to the theatre seemed like special fun. Holding hands or walking arm-in-arm, chatting and laughing, they were a picture perfect young couple in love.

Every night, after the show, they had a meal with friends. After that, Katherine went home and Jeremy went to his cuddlies. However annoying Tommy could be, he brilliantly met Jeremy's physical needs. At any hour of the day or night, Tommy was ready to provide dazzling sexual pleasure.

Thanks to Jeremy's kindness, Katherine was sure of a warm bed, and enough to eat. Stage-door Johnnies constantly courted her, and she accepted a few invitations. Every time a man bought her a meal, he expected sexual favors in return. Every time she refused, the man was furious. The last time she refused to sleep with a casual acquaintance; he slapped her down and left her in the street. After that, she politely refused all invitations. She enjoyed quiet hours alone, writing letters, cleaning the flat, washing and mending their clothes. Someday, she hoped to pay Jeremy back. She owed him so much. For the moment, she was content pretending to be his good little wife.

Chapter Six

December 1889

Henry V finally opened and Jeremy's reviews were excellent. Unfortunately, he was considered just one of many fine repertory actors. The only extraordinary praise came from prissily-clad, heavily lip-rouged theatre critic and tabloid journalist, Archibald Perry.

Obsessed with Jeremy and longing to win his sexual favor, Archie left gifts at the stage-door. He often followed Jerry and his friends into restaurants, and picked up their tabs. When gifts, free meals, and endless flattery failed to win Jeremy's affection, Archie suggested a series of newspaper articles. Jeremy loved that idea and granted him interviews, in very public places. Guessing Jeremy was not actually married, Archie titillated his female readers: one day suggesting that the handsome young actor was a devoted husband, and the next day implying that he was still an eligible bachelor. The tabloid sheets sold out as soon as they were distributed. Fan mail poured into the stage-door and *Henry V* sold out. David Tyler was delighted. Katherine enjoyed playing the celebrity wife, standing proudly by, as strangers stopped her "husband," and asked for autographs.

Archie was still ignored, and angry. He had made Jeremy into a star. He expected compensation.

One freezing predawn, Tommy, Neil, and Jeremy stumbled out of a private club onto a dimly lit street. Shivering with cold, laughing drunk, their breath thick as frozen smoke, they burst into a raucous:

"Hail, hail, the gang's all here!
What the hell do we care?
What the hell do we care…?"

Two tired Bobbies turned a corner and slowly walked toward them. Before Jeremy could warn Tommy, he pressed Neil against the wall and kissed him on the mouth. The Bobbies doubled their speed.

"Oi, there! Wha's this, then?" Tommy and Neil lurched apart, suddenly sober, and terrified. The Bobbies placed themselves on either side, blocking their escape. "All right, you lot. Magistrate will deal with you in the morning." They pulled manacles from their belts, cuffed Tommy, then Neil.

Before Jeremy knew what was happening, one of the Bobbies swung him around and slammed iron cuffs onto his wrists. Wincing with pain, he stared at Tommy struggling to get loose, and Neil collapsed onto the pavement, crying.

The second Bobby sneered with disgust and pulled Neil to his feet. "Bloody pervert. Hope the magistrate locks you up for a long time. The streets are cleaner without you scum."

Tommy stooped low, watching for a chance to bolt. "We haven't done anything wrong."

"Wai' a minute." The first Bobbie pushed his nightstick under Jeremy's chin, and forced his face into the harsh beam of a streetlight. "I know you."

Tommy yelled, "We're actors, damn it. You know all of us."

The Bobby stared. "Why, it's Mr. O'Connell, righ'? Watcha doin' with these pieces of filth then, when y' go' that pretty little wife waitin' at 'ome, eh?" He lowered his nightstick and raised an eyebrow.

Jeremy stood frozen with fear. His wrists and shoulders throbbed and his chin stung. The Bobby looked to his partner, gave a wink, and unlocked Jeremy's handcuffs. He heaved a sigh of relief, rubbed his chafed wrists, and waited for them to release Tommy and Neil.

Instead, the Bobby nudged him with his nightstick. "Go 'ome to yer missus. From now on though, mind the company y' keep."

Tommy's face was defiant. Neil pleaded for help, but Jeremy could do nothing for either one. He hesitated just a moment longer, then ran for his life.

Tommy lurched after him and the Bobby grabbed his arms, wrenching them upwards. "None o' that now."

Jeremy reached a dark alley, hid from view, and looked back. Other club patrons had gathered around.

"Nothin' to see 'ere. Be about yer business." The Bobbies pulled Tommy and Neil through the crowd. "Come on you lot."

After the crowd dispersed, tabloid journalist Archibald Perry stood alone in the alley. A grim smile spread his disgustingly rouged lips. Jeremy's knees gave way and he slumped back against a cold brick wall. Tonight, for the first time in weeks, Archie smiled.

Katherine woke when the door to the flat opened, slammed shut, and locked. "Jerry? What are you doing? ...Jerry?"

Frozen with fear, he stood pressed against the back of the door. A match sputtered and flamed as she lit a candle at her bedside.

"What's happened? Are you injured?" She hurried to him.

He gasped for breath. "Tommy and Neil were arrested. Damn Tommy! I cautioned him a hundred times. We were drunk. He kissed Neil right in front of two coppers."

"Oh, no. What will happen to them?"

"Maximum sentence for gross indecency is two years at hard labor. Thank God they were only kissing. They should get off with much less. Upper-class men aren't fit enough to survive two years..." He broke into quiet sobs.

Katherine stayed calm. "Are you in danger?"

He shook his head. "One of the coppers knew me. He thinks I'm married." He clung to her, holding on for dear life. Remembering all the times she embraced him and he barely tolerated her, he felt ashamed to need her so completely.

Calm and controlled, she brewed him a cup of strong, very sweet tea, made him undress, and get into bed. She held him until he fell asleep.

Five hours later, disguised as a skivvy, Katherine sat with other pitiable men and women enjoying free warmth and entertainment in the gallery of the Court of Petty Sessions. She raced home and told him about the trial.

*

Two white-wigged, black-robed magistrates listened, as two exhausted Bobbies described Tommy and Neil performing an indecent act on a public street. Tommy pleaded guilty. Neil pleaded not guilty, insisting that Tommy assaulted him. Tommy did not react to the accusation, so Katherine guessed the two had planned Neil's defense. The Bobbies could not swear that Neil was lying, and he was released with a caution.

Without a look back, Neil sped from the courtroom, and London. A day later, he sent a letter saying he was sailing for Boston.

The magistrates conferred for only a minute before turning back to Tommy. One spoke. "Thomas Quinn, we esteem yours to be a light offense with grave cause for concern. Indecent behavior in any degree must be regarded as a threat to the entire moral structure of the empire. As such, we remand you to Reading Gaol for a term of five months at hard labor."

Katherine slid from the courtroom and hurried home.

*

All that day Jeremy stayed in the flat. Katherine bought the morning and midday papers, but there was nothing about Tommy or Neil. He waited until the last possible moment, then stuck close to Katherine, and hurried to the theatre. As they approached the Strand, a paperboy shouted, "'*Actor Jailed*!' Get cher paper here."

The next corner was Norfolk Street. A different paper boy waved his sheet. "'*Actor Jeremy O'Connell -- friend of Tommy Quinn: Prince Hal or Prince Pouf?*'... Buy a paper, mister?" Jeremy's face went gray. He lowered his head and plowed on.

Almost at Howard Street, they heard, "'*Scandal at the Strand Theatre!*'" A woman bought the paper. "Yes, madam, 'ere y' are."

Jeremy clutched Katherine's hand, and raced for the stage-door. A heckler recognized him. "Bloody pouf! You should be in jail with yer mates!"

A woman called, "Hiding behind a woman's skirt, are y'? Is that the kind o' man y' are?"

Katherine froze. Jeremy put a protective arm around her, glanced back, and saw Archibald Perry hand each of the hecklers a coin.

The next few days, Jeremy stuck to Katherine like glue. Dreadfully guilty that he was walking free, while terrified he would be found out and pitched into jail with Tommy, he played the ideal husband, staying home every night. At first he missed his friends. Soon, he was enjoying his long nights with Katherine. Lounging in dressing gowns and sipping wine, they shared theatre stories, and read plays aloud.

Jeremy had had a formal education. He was nearly fluent in Greek and Latin. Katherine eagerly listened to his explanations of myths and other references used by great playwrights. She had a quick mind and peppered him with questions. By the end of the second week, he was hurrying her home so they could study late into the night. They developed insights for

33

the classic characters they hoped to play, and Jeremy suddenly longed to produce his own plays. He wanted to control everything on-stage and backstage. His fondness for Katherine grew into respect, then admiration.

Katherine's skills as an actress improved so quickly, her first performance as Titania was better than the veteran actress she understudied. When Jeremy told her, she was ecstatic.

Living on top of each other, in one-and-a-half rooms, made physical modesty impossible. Jeremy loved looking at Katherine's body. He adored her beautiful legs, tight little bottom, and firm breasts. One night they changed into their night clothes, and he made the mistake of saying, "Someone should sculpt you, Katie. Your shape is absolutely perfect."

She dropped her nightdress and stood naked. "Your body is beautiful, too. I could look at you forever." He was vain enough to believe her, but also wary. Before he could end the conversation, she said, "Our bodies might fit. Really, they might. We never even tried." She looked so beautiful and so hopeful, he felt like a cad.

Needing to end this, he dropped his nightshirt and stood naked. "My darling girl, any nice regular chap would take one look at you, grow to the size of Big Ben, and ravish you on the spot. As you can see, my tiny acorn cringes with embarrassment." Humiliated, he turned away and pulled his nightshirt over his head. "I am so sorry, Katie. You deserve better."

"N' No, I'm sorry -- truly -- You're the finest man in the entire world." She threw her nightdress over her head and covered herself. "I'll never mention it again. I promise."

He sighed, and quoted the bard, *"Come Kate, we'll to bed,"* snuffed the candle, and climbed under the covers. Streetlight sneaked through the drapes as she moved in next to him. He held her tight, kissed her soft lips, and suddenly found himself on top of her, kissing her deeply. He felt wonderful. Just as suddenly, his passion cooled. He lay down, turned over, and waited for her to snuggle against his back.

Instead, she leaned on her elbow, touched his shoulder, and ran a light finger down his arm. "Jerry?" Her breathing was labored. "I'm... That is..." Nervous as a cat, she forced out, "When I was with Simon, we didn't always..." She geared up her courage and started again. "I mean, well... he taught me some... things...,"

He burst out laughing. "I'm sure he taught you a great many things."

She laughed with him, and gently covered his face with light kisses. Slowly, she unbuttoned his nightshirt, and folded it back so that he lay naked. Her soft hands glided over his very willing flesh, as she kissed his neck and shoulders. Her golden hair draped, as her lips moved softly across his chest and down his belly. Fingertips light as dove feathers wound around his slender organ. She caressed him with absolute affection and tenderness. His eyes closed and his back arched with delight.

Hoping against hope that he had actually grown to a serviceable size, he glanced down and saw that he was still very small. He gasped when she took him into her mouth, caressing with her delicate tongue. All at once, he clutched the pillow, groaned, heaved backward, and lay still. He dozed off and, moments later, was thrilled by the sensation of a warm cloth wiping him clean. Katie returned her washcloth to the basin and snuggled against him, under the warm quilt.

Still reeling from her unexpected skill, and pure unselfish love, he held her close and kissed the top of her lovely head. Longing to pleasure her, the way she had thrilled him, he stroked her shoulder, then her small, shapely breast. She gasped happily, so he caressed her soft nipple, feeling it harden under his fingertips. Her nightdress was a single piece without buttons, so she pulled it off, over her head. They lay together, naked for the first time.

He kissed her nipples until they both stood firm and hard. She moaned and closed her eyes, just as he had done when she caressed him. His fingers wandered to her nether regions, but he felt like a voyager without a map. She had had an able tutor, but he was delving into uncharted territory.

Katherine was not a bit shy about directing his fingers. He enjoyed the tour, thinking he might discover that delectable "honey pot," often praised by the great bards. He was amazed to find soft, curly blond hair and the silkiest flesh in the world. Her golden hairs reminded him of Simon's, and he imagined the beautiful children they could make together. She guided his fingers until one lingered on a single spot. She held him there, gently rubbing his finger back-and-forth. He continued, and she lay back, smiling. Within seconds, the soft flesh hardened into a round marble. Her legs clamped together, and her face contorted. She cried out, relaxed, and gasped for breath. A light sheen of sweat glimmered on her smooth flesh. Tears glistened in her beautiful eyes.

"You're crying. I've done something wrong."

"No, nothing wrong, darling." She lay back, grinning. "You were perfect."

He rolled his eyes. "Far from 'perfect.' Half the men in London would give their right arm to be in my place, right now. I don't know what's wrong with me. Other poufs have wives. Some have children. Oscar - Bloody - Wilde has *two*. I shall never have any."

Katherine stared at him. "I never knew you wanted children. I certainly don't. I spent most of my life supporting my younger sisters. That was enough mothering for a lifetime."

He tried to smile back, but looked very sad.

She kissed him hard and fast. "You were wonderful. Please believe me. Simon and I often did what we did -- especially in the middle of my cycle, when I was likely to conceive. You pleased me so very much. Honestly."

"I want to believe you."

"Then do." She pulled the covers around them both, and snuggled tight.

Chapter Seven

Prisoners in Reading Gaol were allowed visitors once every three months. A seedy acquaintance managed to bribe an official, and get Jeremy a pass after thirty-three days. Both Katherine and Jeremy irrationally feared that he could walk into the jail and never return. She begged to go with him, or even go in his place.

"Thanks love, but no. If it weren't for Tommy's silence, I would be in prison. I owe him this much." Jeremy knew that Tommy never accepted responsibility for his mistakes. Since Katherine was sleeping in Jeremy's bed, Tommy might irrationally blame her for his arrest.

Once at the prison, Jeremy was given a cursory search, then ushered into an unheated holding area with three-dozen other visitors. Most were women. Most were poor. Jeremy felt conspicuously overdressed, crammed on a rough wooden bench between smutty strangers, breathing stale air, gazing at gray stone walls.

A heavy door clanged open and a warder read a list of names. As Tommy's name was called, Jeremy stood and nearly lost his balance. Clenching his jaw, willing his heart to slow, he treated this like any other performance. Tommy needed him to be strong. He followed the queue into a long, narrow room. A dozen men in poorly fitting prison uniforms were shackled to long tables. The other visitors raced to their husbands, sons, or fathers. Some burst into tears.

It took Jeremy a moment to make out Tommy at the end of the row. His face was gray. Eyes half-closed, elbows leaning heavily on the table, he looked exhausted, filthy, and dangerously thin. His cheeks were so hollow; his crooked tooth looked slightly sinister. His usually fluffy hair was combed back, held solid by its own grease. Razor nicks spotted his face. Jeremy did not suppose prisoners were allowed to handle razors. Someone else must have shaved him.

Jeremy forced a pleasant smile and sauntered down the row. Tommy's smile was joyous. He tried to stand, heaved at his shackles, then jerked back onto the hard bench. Jeremy sat in a sturdy chair on the other side of the table, pretending not to notice that Tommy's nails were chipped and filthy.

Tommy had been under the code of silence, and unable to speak for a month. His voice was a hoarse whisper. "Thanks for coming. Do I look horrible? There aren't any mirrors."

Jeremy lied. "You look fine."

"They're killing me."

Jeremy bent forward. "You are not dying. You will be out of here and I will take care of you."

"You can't. You can't be anywhere near me. You shouldn't even visit. We were lucky with that copper, but...,"

"I'll get you a room. Just as soon as you're well again, we'll see about...,"

"Damn it, Jerry. Go home to that revolting girl and leave me alone. I'm ruined. I'll never work again."

Jeremy's heart skipped a beat, but he hoped his face showed nothing. "You are a fine actor. Of course you will work again."

"Not in Victoria's empire."

"All right then... In someone else's empire." Tommy scowled, and Jeremy hesitated before whispering, "Tell me what it's like."

Tommy shook his head, rubbed his eyes, and looked at his fingers. "Filthy. Everything's filthy and cold. For two weeks, I wore a stinking cloth hood, with holes for eyes, and marched to nowhere, round-and-round a circular yard. There were a hundred men, all in hoods. Every day, marching -- through cold -- drenching rain -- six-hours-a-day. Now, I'm on the treadmill, climbing stairs to nowhere, six-hours-a-day. If I slow, the warders beat me with a truncheon. You can't see my legs and back, but they're all over bruises. My shoes don't fit, so my feet are scabbed and calloused. I used to have such pretty feet."

He sobbed softly. "I sleep on a board with a thin blanket. Sometimes my arms and legs go numb with cold. We get watery cocoa and stale bread for breakfast, soup or a slice of fatty meat is dinner, and a spoonful of suet and potatoes is tea. They march us into chapel every morning and twice on Sundays, but we're not allowed to speak or read anything. Some warders sneak out letters for other prisoners, but none of them like me." He rocked pitifully. "I'm so hungry." Tears rolled down his cheeks.

"Worst is the code of silence. Some days I want to scream. If I even speak, it'll be solitary confinement and the crank."

Exactly twenty minutes after Jeremy's group of visitors was allowed in, they were ushered out. Tearful calls of, "God, bless" "Don't forget me" "Love to the kids" and "Give mum a kiss for me" echoed through the hall. Tommy cried like a frightened child. It took all of Jeremy's acting ability to stay calm. His heart pounded as he followed other visitors from the jail.

Safely through the gate, Jeremy hurried away, down street after street, only stopping when his breath gave out. He leaned against a lamp post, gasping, blinded by tears.

He never asked how it was accomplished, but every Sunday morning he was given a pass and allowed to visit Reading Gaol. Tommy grew so thin and ill, he appeared to age before Jeremy's eyes. Every week, Katherine waited back at the flat with dinner ready. Jeremy always returned upset, angry, full of guilt and self-loathing. She learned to keep silent and out of his way.

One Sunday, he returned early. Without a word, he hung up his coat and hat, and lit a cigarette. His hands shook. He seldom smoked, and never in the flat. Katherine prepared dinner and watched him sit in a chair, smoking cigarette after cigarette.

Finally, her nerves wore thin. "Jerry, what's happened?"

"He fell on the treadmill, cut his leg, cried out, and broke the code of silence. He's in solitary for a month. No visitors." He lit one cigarette from another. "The warder told me there is a crank in his room. He has to turn it ten-thousand-times a day to earn his rations."

Katherine was sure she had misheard. "Ten-*thousand*-times?"

"That is what he said." He sucked the cigarette, blinking back tears.

All this time, The Strand Theatre enjoyed an excellent season. *Henry V* played to full houses and David Tyler was elated. Immediately after Tommy's arrest, hecklers disturbed a few performances, shouting insults from the gallery. Audiences were always noisy, and those few disruptive voices stopped. Jeremy assumed Archibald Perry had stopped paying them.

Katherine and Jeremy continued living in counterfeit wedded bliss.

Enjoying their charade, Simon Camden now addressed his letters to Mr. and Mrs. Jeremy O'Connell. He even sent a new photo of himself that hung on their wall. His inscription read,

To Jerry and Kathy,
The world's finest couple!
All my love,
Simon Camden

The letters arrived as regular as clockwork, always funny, always filled with randy adventures, always ending with pledges of eternal love for Katherine.

Winter brightened into spring, then summer, and Jeremy began counting the days until Tommy's release. One cool Sunday morning in June, he left the flat while Katherine prepared a leg of mutton, vegetables, potatoes, and Yorkshire pudding. He returned looking tense, but smiling, and hung up his coat.

"Twelve more days and Tommy's a free man. I'll collect his clothes from the theatre storeroom, then move him into a boarding house. He'll need food, towels, shaving soap... When he's well enough to work..."

"But, you said that no theatre will hire him, that the scandal will follow him for the rest of his life."

"He will never work as an actor. He will have to find some other employment. God knows what. He's been on the stage since he was a boy. He's even a rather lazy actor. He'll hate working a regular trade."

She looked concerned. "You haven't funds enough to keep us all. You must allow me to pay my share." He hesitated long enough for her to say, "Please, Jerry. My family's doing better, their engagements are coming nicely. It seems my sister has finally learned to dance."

He sighed and nodded. "Thank you. And that mutton smells divine." He kissed the top of her head, noticed a pile of unopened mail, and moved to the desk.

She scowled thoughtfully. "And I'll move Tommy's things into the boarding house. All the 'cuddlies,' as you call them, refuse to admit they even know him, and you mustn't be seen with him."

"Unfortunately, you are correct. I shall have to let you."

40

"I'll stay as long as you need to pretend we're married, but I can afford my own digs now." She checked the meat, and hesitated before asking, "Do you want me to stay?"

"Good grief! Of course I do… and not just for show. I love your being here. I'm eating proper meals. My clothes have never looked better." He put his tongue in his cheek and she laughed with relief. All at once, he lunged across the room, took her in his arms, and kissed her. When the kiss ended, he held her tight and gazed at her lovely face.

The days leading up to Tommy's release found hecklers revisiting The Strand Theatre. Every few performances, Jeremy recited a line and was answered by a snide remark from the gallery, or now even more boldly, from the stalls. Ticket sales were still excellent. David Tyler watched the situation, but did nothing.

Tommy's final night in prison, Jeremy was backstage dressed as King Henry. Katherine and other actors in Elizabethan costumes stood backstage listening for their cues. A newspaper lay on the prop table. The headline read: *ACTOR TOMMY QUINN RELEASED TOMORROW.*

One of the actors whispered through clenched teeth, "Bloody scavengers. Haven't they sucked enough out of him?"

An old actress hissed, "It was big news when he was arrested, and it's big news now he's getting out."

David Tyler walked tensely through the wings, then gazed into the stalls.

Jeremy walked on stage and spoke his first line, "*Where is my gracious lord of Canterbury?*"

From a box overhanging the stage, a heckler shouted, "Maybe he's in Reading Gaol, where y' ought t' be!" Other hecklers laughed.

The actor playing Exeter continued, "*Not here in presence.*"

"Hidin' out in yer love nest?" shouted a shrill female voice.

Jeremy turned to the actor playing Westmorland. "*Send for him, good uncle.*"

The actor answered, "*Shall I call the ambassador, my liege?*"

"Call 'im a flamin' pouf!" sounded from a new male voice.

Katherine peered out to see the hecklers, as Jeremy continued, "*Not yet, my cousin…*"

"And there's his beard!" The first heckler pointed gleefully at Katherine. "He's pretendin' to be married to that bit o' skirt."

Tyler pulled Katherine back, shouting, "Lower the curtain. Now!" There was confusion as the curtain flew down and actors scrambled to get out of its way. Tyler was furious. "Filthy bastards. It's gotten worse every performance."

Jeremy stood flushed, breathing hard. "I'm sorry Mr. Tyler. I suggest you start the play again, this time with Kevin Killen. He knows the role." Everyone stared at Jeremy, then his young understudy playing a servant. Kevin's mouth dropped open.

Tyler knew Kevin was prepared. "Are you sure this is what you want?"

Jeremy shrugged. "It's that or refund the entire audience. I'll get out of London for a while, tour the provinces."

Katherine paled. "But what will I...?"

Tyler shouted instructions. "Mr. O'Connell, Miss Stewart, wait in my office -- Mr. Killen, change your costume -- Fred, reset for the top of the scene -- Now!" There was a flurry of activity as Tyler pushed the curtain aside and strode onto the apron. Katherine and Jeremy hurried off-stage as Tyler addressed the audience.

"Ladies and Gentlemen. For the remainder of tonight's performance, the role of King Henry will be played by a brilliant young actor, Mr. Kevin Killen." An equal number of cheers and boos came from the audience.

Half-an-hour later, Katherine looked as if her life was over. David Tyler counted out money, and Jeremy pleaded, "The season's only another three weeks, surely Katie can stay."

He shook his head. "I can't trust the hecklers to leave her alone. I'm sorry."

The next afternoon, Tommy walked out of Reading Gaol. Katherine found him a room near the docks. Every few days she brought him food, washed and mended his clothes. He and Jeremy met secretly in filthy alleyways and out-of-the-way pubs. Jeremy expected him to be ill and depressed for a while, but the days progressed, his appearance returned to near normal, and his mood remained sullen. The only thing that made him smile was money, so Jeremy gave him more than he could afford. Sure that Tommy would not find theatre work, Jeremy begged him to learn some other trade. He refused. Every day he visited theatrical casting offices, just to be turned away.

Jeremy was unemployed and at his wits' end. The sudden offer of an open-ended tour through the North Country, Scotland, and Wales was a godsend. Not only would it take him away from the tabloids, the hecklers, and Tommy Quinn, but for the first time, he would be playing only leading roles. The wage was triple what he earned at The Strand. He was thrilled.

Katherine offered to stay as Tommy's child-minder, but Jeremy forbad it. "Tommy's intelligent and resourceful. He'll do fine, as soon as you stop coddling him and I stop paying him off."

As much as Jeremy would miss Katherine, he knew their separation was good. She would have a chance to meet men. She was beautiful and charming, but he never expected her to be fearless, intelligent, and nurturing. She had become his best friend. He relied on her. He adored her.

The morning Jeremy left London, Katherine sat in an armchair, glared at his trunk, and sipped milky tea. She always took sugar, hadn't today, and was too upset to notice.

Busy at his desk, he wrote a letter, folded a wide five-pound-note with some coins inside the paper, then put it all into an envelope. "I'm posting the rent, so you can keep the flat straight through the summer."

Katherine gulped the rest of her tea. "I know you have no concern for your safety, but you need to protect yourself. You should marry me... really marry me."

He sighed, long and hard. "After what Tommy has suffered, I can never live that lie."

"But you care for me. It would not be a lie."

"Caring for someone and being in love are very different. I could never fall in love with a woman."

She sobbed and dropped her teacup.

It crashed to the floor and he rushed to clean the mess. "I'm sorry, darling. When I'm gone, you can find a nice man who will treat you properly... Make you feel like a woman."

She choked out, "Nice men don't keep company with actresses. Besides, I don't care about... that."

"You should care, and you will care about it very much, with the right chap." He laughed sadly. "Darling, you need to stay in London to start making a name for yourself. You have had more than enough tour experience and you are good enough to get a principal engagement. I am sure you will have a wonderful career, but you need to work, to hone your craft."

Two hours later, she tearfully waved good-bye as his train pulled out of King's Cross Station.

Fleeing London, Archibald Perry, his tabloids, his hecklers, and Tommy Quinn felt like escaping hell. As soon as the train rolled out of town, into the lush countryside, his relief transformed into gnawing guilt. He had just deserted Katherine. Simon had deserted her the same way, less than a year before. Of course, their situations were totally different. He had had no choice, but still... He asked a porter for pen and paper, and started the first of a hundred letters he would send her. She answered promptly and their connection stayed as strong as if they were still living under one roof. For the first time since he was a schoolboy, he knew that one person on God's green earth loved him unconditionally.

Chapter Eight

July 1892

For Jeremy O'Connell, the next three years flew fast as dry leaves in an autumn wind. Physically exhausted, sexually euphoric, and artistically rewarded, Jeremy worked with more energy and commitment than he ever thought possible. He played good theatres, and leading roles. He tried new methods of acting, playing the same role in different styles. He thought some of his performances were utter rubbish that London audiences would have crucified. Provincial audiences were forgiving, and he learned from his mistakes. He honed his technique, and became the fine actor he always dreamed he could be.

Other actors in the company asked his advice and he taught them, as the same way he had taught Katherine. When he played London again, he would become a teacher, as well as an actor-manager, and stage his own plays. The problem was: how to get hold of a London theatre. On tour, he made excellent wages and pulled in large audiences. One theatrical broadsheet read:

JEREMY O'CONNELL: TOP EARNER IN THE PROVINCES

Simon Camden had become an actor-manager. During the off-season, he rented sets and costumes from Henry Irving, engaged his own company, and toured ratty village theatres too small to afford star actors. His letters were always entertaining.

Dear Jerry,

A sweet little bird's taking care of me just now, but I wish it were Kathy…

If all goes according to plan, my future is guaranteed. Who would have guessed that Her Majesty's armed forces would be eager for highbrow entertainment? They long for legitimate theatre, and have engaged me to present it. I have inflated my budget almost double and, short a disaster, in five years I will have played every role I ever dreamed of, seen most of Victoria's empire, and I will come home a wealthy man.

Jeremy pictured brash and beautiful Simon Camden, costumed like a gentleman, charming stuffy military officers into giving him anything he wanted. The letter continued:

...Tommy Quinn was desperate for work, so I got a first-class actor at half what he is worth...

Jeremy caught his breath. Long ago, Tommy had disappeared from London. Jeremy had no desire to see him, but wished him well. He was delighted Simon was keeping him employed on the other side of the planet. As always, Simon ended by writing about Katherine.

... I wish Kathy would join my tour. Then everything would be perfect. I cannot believe she is still working for Eric Bates. He is a nice chap, but soooo dull.

Katherine was also doing well.

Darling Jerry,

I have been employed by a new actor-manager, Eric Bates. Do you know him? Simon acted with him on tour.

Mr. Bates is married to a rich wife who leased him a small theatre. Hilda Bates does not appreciate her husband's craft, disrupts rehearsals, and demands that he attend social functions he despises. They have two sweet little girls.

Mr. Bates is soft spoken, kind and patient. Sadly, he has little imagination and no technique. He is quite a good actor in character roles, but not handsome. He often casts himself as the leading man, which does not suit.

The first production is Twelfth Night, *and I play Viola. Mr. Bates prepared a detailed staging chart, moving us like chess pieces, with one move for every spoken line. It was dreadful, of course, and he tossed it out. Now, he lets us do whatever we please, and that is equally dreadful. Some actors are outrageously slapstick, some are melodramatic, and others are absurdly introspective.*

As principal actress, I am receiving brilliant reviews and the same fine treatment I remember as a headline dancer in Variety.

Jerry darling, you are a better actor than either Simon or Eric Bates. You say you will not come back to London until you can lease a theatre, but Simon had to leave the continent and Eric had to marry a harridan to find that much money. I fear there is no other way.

Please come home. I have changed nothing in the flat, and miss you terribly.

Katherine wrote regularly and each time mentioned Eric Bates. At first he was, "Mr. Bates." Eventually he became, "Eric," and finally, "Darling Eric." Jeremy could not be sure, but guessed they were having an affair. Play after play, the reviewers raved about her and panned Darling Eric's productions. Audiences stayed away in droves. Jeremy encouraged her to move on, but she was determined to stay with Darling Eric. Jeremy was about to sign a contract for another touring season when a telegram arrived.

ERIC DESPERATE -- STOP -- WIFE CLOSING THEATRE UNLESS NEXT SEASON SUCCESS -- STOP -- OFFERS YOU ONE PRODUCTION TO STAGE -- STOP -- MUST ACT IN THREE OF HIS -- STOP -- PAY SAME AS STRAND – STOP

Without hesitation he wired back:

ARRIVING LONDON FIFTEEN DAYS -- STOP -- WANT SHREW – STOP

Immediately after sending the telegram, he wrote Katherine a long letter giving his arrival time and describing the entire *Taming Of The Shrew* he staged in his imagination. They would be brilliant together. He was bursting to begin rehearsals, return to his lovely little flat, and the arms of his darling girl. He began focusing on the success he so desperately wanted and knew he could achieve.

TONIGHT AT 8:00 200th PERFORMANCE
Mr. JEREMY O'CONNELL
Miss KATHERINE STEWART
In THE TAMING OF THE SHREW

At eight-fifteen, Darling Eric's wife, Hilda Bates, gleefully tallied the evening's receipts. The sold-out audience howled with laughter as Petruchio twisted Kate's arm behind her back.

"Who knows not where a wasp does wear his sting?

In his tail."

"In his tongue."

"Whose tongue?"

"Yours if you talk of tails: and so farewell." Katherine thrashed violently as Jeremy pressed his front up against her back.

"What. With my tongue in your tail?"

Katherine kicked behind her, appearing to strike him in the groin. He lurched back in pretend pain, and the audience howled once more.

Two hours later, the audience rose to their feet, cheering. Jeremy stood center-stage with Katherine on one side and Eric, dressed as her father Baptista, on the other. A dozen more actors spread out on either side as they bowed and smiled, again-and-again.

When the curtain-call finally ended, Eric raised his hands to heaven. "Two-hundred sold out performances and three other plays doing nearly as well. Soon we'll need a bigger theatre. Thank you, God. Thank you, Jerry."

He pumped Jeremy's hand and hugged Katherine. She leaned against him and gazed adoringly at Jeremy. Several handsomely dressed young men appeared in the wings. Jeremy waved and went to join them. Katherine gazed sadly after him as he left the stage.

Katherine and Jeremy had slipped back to a comfortable routine. They both made decent salaries and could easily afford a larger flat. Moving house was a nuisance, so they never bothered. They did engage a maid-of-all-work to do the cleaning and washing up. Most nights Jeremy stayed out late, but still loved coming home to Katherine. As much as he preached that she should find a nice regular chap, he was secretly delighted that very married Darling Eric Bates was serving her womanly requirements.

One night, Jeremy left his dressing room flanked by two handsome young admirers. "Jerry!" Katherine smiled at the young men and pulled him away, whispering frantically. "I'm sorry, but there's something I've got to discuss with you. Please stay, just for a minute."

She looked very upset, but he gestured toward his guests. "I promised the lads...,"

"Please. I'd never ask if it wasn't urgent." There were tears in her eyes.

He turned to the young men. "Go ahead chaps. I'll catch you up. Order whatever you like, just put it on my tab."

Katherine led Jeremy into her dressing room and shut the door. He waited, coat on, hat in hand, as she leaned on the dressing table, breathing hard. "I'm carrying a child and I have to get rid of it. Eric mustn't be told."

Jeremy was stunned. "But... he has to be told."

"Our affair is scandal enough. Hilda has twice threatened to divorce him."

"Would that be bad? He loves you. He'll marry you, if you want him."

She swung around. "Of course it would be bad. He'll lose the theatre. Fifty people will lose their positions and his daughter's reputations will be ruined. Please darling, you know people... doctors."

He stared at her. "I do not know any butchers."

"There are good doctors who do this. They're expensive, but...,"

"It is too dangerous. I will not hear of it."

They were silent for a few minutes. Slowly, Jeremy's lips spread into a mischievous smile. "I don't really know why you are so concerned. If you recall, half the tabloids report that you are married to me."

She sneered, "The other half 'report' that you're a pouf and I'm a harlot. Help me."

"All right. I'll help you." He tossed his hat on a chair. "I will see you through the birth of this child. Give the baby away if you must, but do not give your life over to a butcher."

They were both silent. Beginning to sweat, Jeremy took off his coat and studied her. A happy excitement sent his heart racing. "Katie -- Marry me -- Really."

"That's the daftest suggestion of all."

"You know I adore children. I've longed to have one of my own. I never thought I could."

She was appalled. "You're actually serious... What about your -- young men?"

"This has nothing to do with them." He put his hands on her shoulders. "I will take care of you and the child. You will never lack for anything.

Not ever." His face was close to hers. Tears rolled down her cheeks and he thought his heart would break.

"Oh, Jerry, you were wonderful the last time I needed you. But that was temporary. Raising a child is a commitment, for years and years."

"I know. Won't it be fun."

Chapter Nine

Yorkshire: October 1896

"Whoa, Billy!" Elisa Roundtree nearly slid off the back of her shaggy highland pony. Riding without saddle or bridle, she straightened up, gripped her strong, short legs around his smooth belly, and reached wiry arms around his neck. Pulling his head to one side, she steered him away from a dangerous gully. Once all four hoofs were on solid ground, she pulled on his mane. He obediently stopped, then impatiently shook his head.

She patted his neck, laughing affectionately. "Silly pony. You could have broken a leg and dropped me in the mud."

She hugged his neck, and pulled a sugar cube from her pocket. Once again, she gripped her legs, stretched her arm, and reached low enough so he could take it with his soft lips.

"It's all right. You're still my best friend." He whinnied in agreement. She laughed, scratching his ear. "I know you want to run, but we have to get off this sinking marsh."

She gripped his mane, gently squeezed his sides with her knees, and eased him forward. "Just go slowly to the top of the ridge, Billy. Then we can gallop home." Her sharp eyes watched every inch of soggy ground, and kept the pony winding along a safe path. Once they reached the hilltop, a half-mile from the estate, she put her face against the pony's neck.

"Go! Billy, go!" Pony and rider bolted as one. Elisa's long matted hair blended with the pony's mane, blowing wildly against the wind. Her small body swayed with Billy and the rhythmic beat of his pounding hoofs.

They were almost at the house before Elisa noticed the black motor car. Three figures stood on the porch. *Oh, no!* Wishing she could turn Billy back, she closed her eyes the rest of the way. Her heart raced as Billy slowed enough to enter the stable without injuring them both.

The groom unceremoniously pulled Elisa off the pony's back. "Yer in for it now, Missie. They've been callin' y' fer hours."

Elisa looked herself over and shuddered. She wore torn boots, jodhpurs, and a stable boy's tight weave coat. Her hands and face were splattered with dried mud. On the porch, her father Anthony Roundtree gripped the railing. He was dressed in one of his best suits and his face was red with rage.

"Elisa! Come here at once. You were told Sir John was visiting, today. You deliberately disobeyed….,"

"I didn't father. Honestly. I forgot." She ran up the stoop, stopped just out of his reach, and curtsied. "I am very sorry, father."

She turned to Sir John Garingham. "How-do-you-do, Sir John? I beg your pardon for being late."

Her father's friend glowered as Elisa curtsied again, this time banging her heavy boot on the wood planking. The unladylike sound made her cowering Aunt Lillian whimper and cover her mouth.

"It's all right, Aunt. I haven't caught cold." Her spinster aunt's frightened expression warned that Elisa was in deep trouble.

Her father took a menacing step forward, and Elisa lurched back against the porch rail. "You'll catch far more than a cold, my girl."

He reached for her, but she sped past him, into the house and upstairs to her room. She slammed the door and reached to turn the key. It was gone. Her father's heavy footsteps pounded up the stairs. She heard a key go into the keyhole from the other side and turn. Her father's footsteps started again, first loud then softer as he hurried back downstairs. She tried the door. It held fast. She heard the car engine start up, threw open a window and leaned out. Below, she could see Sir John berating her father.

"Two days, Roundtree. Do you hear me?"

Roundtree wiped sweat off his brow. "Yes, Sir John, two days. I promise."

Sir John climbed into his car, motioning for the chauffeur to drive away.

Elisa pulled herself back inside, closed the window, and slumped onto the floor. Two days? What's happening in two days? Her stomach growled, but she knew she would go hungry as punishment. Cook used to sneak her food. Then her father threatened to sack any servant who disobeyed his orders.

Elisa often climbed down the trellis to steal food from the pantry. When she was caught she got a beating... Suddenly cold, she shivered, stood up and stared at her reflection in the mirror.

"I look like a tramp." She grabbed a comb, stuck it into her hair, and pulled. "Ouch!" The comb did not move. Determined, she tried again. This time, the comb lowered an inch and stopped. When she took her hand away, the comb stayed, sticking out from her head. She laughed at the silly sight, then soberly put the comb back on the dresser. She sat on her bed, watching the trees outside her window fade, then disappear into the black night. Tired, hungry, lonely, and frightened, she kicked off her boots and curled up in a quilt. What will happen in two days?

*

Pony Billy whinnied in distress and Elisa woke with a start. She tried the door. It was still bolted. She raced to a window, threw a leg over the sill onto the trellis, then climbed down the sturdy rose canes. She ignored the thorns piercing her bare feet, jumped the last yard, and ran around the corner of the house. The pony was being driven away in a cart.

"No!" She screamed and ran after him.

Her arm was nearly wrenched from its socket as she flipped backward, face to face with Sir John Garingham. He grabbed her other arm, lifted her off the ground and slammed her down again. She winced with pain, too frightened to make a sound.

Sir John visited every year, but had never spoken to Elisa. Now his face was inches above hers. She could see pores in his skin and stains on his teeth. His voice was a threatening rumble. "From today, you will learn to be a lady."

He threw her at her father. She cried out as Anthony Roundtree dragged her inside, and downstairs to the kitchen. The maid, footman, and cook stood tensely. Hearing the commotion, her Aunt Lillian Roundtree scurried down the stairs, still in her nightdress.

Roundtree shoved Elisa toward his sister. "Lillian, I want her scrubbed and her hair combed. The governess arrives tomorrow."

Elisa pleaded, "Please father, where have you taken Billy?"

"That wild beast has gone to auction. If you ever ride again, it will be on a proper lady's mount, with a sidesaddle." He stomped up the stairs.

Elisa stared after him. "Billy's gone to auction? A sidesaddle?"

Lillian, frail and shivering, started to cry. A young maid handed her a handkerchief. "There, there, Miss Lillian, mustn't let your brother bother you so. You know the way he is. Let's just get you dressed..." She gently pushed wisps of graying red hair away from her mistress's face, and led her upstairs. Lillian followed like an obedient child.

Elisa watched the strong footman fill a large pan with water and put it on a back burner to boil. He and the cook pulled the iron bathtub from its hooks on the wall.

The cook gave Elisa a glass of milk. She drank it down and asked for more. The cook laughed as she poured more milk, then wiped the white moustache from Elisa's upper lip. "Sit luv, y' had no dinner." The cook broke two eggs into a sizzling pan of grease, then put a thick slice of bread to toast over the fire. The eggs crackled and minutes later, the cook dipped the toast into a bowl of drippings. She put the toast onto a plate and flipped the orange yoked eggs on top of it. Elisa gratefully devoured it all.

After breakfast, Elisa was deposited in a tub of hot water. An able house maid scrubbed her clean. A hopeless bundle of nerves, her Aunt Lillian stood to the side, fussing with the lace on her cuffs, pulling at her copper curls, and talking nonsense.

Cleaning did little to improve the girl's chewed and calloused fingers. Her naturally coarse light red hair was washed with a strong solution of hemp root, maiden vine, soft cabbage cores, and honey. After it was rinsed, two full cups of lanolin were needed to soften it for combing. Elisa cried, as the maid and the cook took turns inching combs through the tangles. Some were so bad they needed to be cut out. When they finished, a full three inches had been trimmed off the bottom of her now bright copper locks.

To avoid her hair tangling again, it was parted in the middle and pulled into two tight braids. Finally, dressed in an everyday frock and high-button-shoes, Elisa watched her old boots and britches get tossed into the fire.

"But, what will I play in, Aunt? I can't go onto the moors like this."

Lillian wrung her hands. "You're not to go on the moors, dearest. You're to stay in the house and become a lady." She proudly patted her coiffed copper hair, delicately streaked with gray. "You'll have your hair combed every day. You'll stay clean and learn proper manners."

"But ladies don't do anything." Elisa reached under her skirt, trying to loosen a tight garter.

"Stop that!" Lillian pulled the skirt back over Elisa's knees. "Please child. You have always worn frocks to church. Now you must wear them every day. You won't mind, after a while. Sir John is adamant. We must do as he wishes."

"Why aunt? Why must we do as he wishes?"

"No questions, child. Young ladies must be seen and not heard."

"But...,"

"Silence!"

The next day, Anthony Roundtree and his sister stood stiff and silent. Elisa, dressed in her best clothes, was marched into the drawing room to meet the governess. Afraid of doing anything wrong, Elisa glanced up at the dour woman in black, then stood perfectly still, with her feet primly together and her hands at her sides. She looked very pretty. Sir John was pleasantly surprised. He spoke to the governess as though Elisa were not in the room.

"She looks sweet enough, Kimball, but you mustn't be deceived. She's a hellcat."

Kimball raised her long nose and spoke with singsong condescension. "I trained your three nephews, My Lord. One little girl will hardly prove a challenge."

Elisa hated her. She knew men could be cruel. Women had always been kind to her. This woman was different.

Sir John raised one thick eyebrow. "I hope you are right. I'm touring the mines then going abroad. In six months I'll return." He stood and everyone jumped to attention. "Kimball, if you can do what you say, you will be well rewarded. Good day to you all... Roundtree, a word." Roundtree followed Sir John out.

Kimball turned to Lillian. "I will take complete responsibility for the child, Miss Roundtree. You need not trouble with her from now on. It's best if she does not see you at all for the first month."

Elisa's stomach cramped violently. Her eyes went wide.

Lillian opened her mouth to speak, but was cut off.

"After the first month, if you wish, she may be presented once a day, perhaps at tea time."

Elisa's pleading eyes forced her aunt to speak. "What about Sunday services, Miss Kimball?"

Kimball glared. "You are Anglicans, I suppose?"

Lillian shrugged in despair.

Elisa thought of kind Father Folen and the sweets he gave her after services. He let her talk as much as she pleased. Other adults scolded that she should be seen and not heard. When the church was empty, Lillian stayed to gossip with Mrs. Folen and other ladies.

Kimball rolled her eyes. "Very well. You will tell me what time she must be readied. I trust there is a Catholic Church in your village?"

"Oh, yes, just down the…,"

"Fine. I shall attend mass. Immediately after, the child must be returned to me."

Elisa and Lillian sighed with relief.

"Miss Roundtree."

Lillian jumped. "Yes, Miss Kimball."

"Be so kind as to show me to my room and have tea and sandwiches sent up. When I am refreshed, I shall visit the nursery. Miss Elisa, you will show me your embroidery and your penmanship."

Elisa's mouth fell open. "Pardon Miss, but I haven't done either."

Kimball stiffened. "Surely you can read and write."

"I read all the time, Miss. But I haven't written much, and I don't like embroidery."

The governess clenched her jaw. "Well, perhaps Sir John was right. You will be a challenge after all."

Elisa nervously bit her finger.

"Show me your hands."

She tentatively held them up.

Kimball turned them back and front, looking at the chewed nails. "I shall break you of that habit, this week."

Chapter Ten

Elisa bent over her study desk, copying the endless lines in her penmanship book. She was unaware of raising her left hand and slipping a fingernail between her teeth. *Whoosh!* The sting of Miss Kimball's switch flicked across her hand. Shaking the stinging hand, Elisa returned it to the desk top. Knowing tears would earn her an extra stroke, she blinked furiously and continued her work. When she bent too far over her book, *Whoosh!* The switch struck her shoulder, making her sit up straight.

After penmanship, came embroidery. Elisa believed that she might, someday, want to write someone a letter, but she knew that she would never want to decorate a handkerchief. Unfortunately, needlework was Kimball's passion. She was determined that Elisa have something to show Sir John, when he returned. Elisa found complicated stitches fun to learn, but boring to repeat. Sloppy stitches were pulled out and re-sewn. A third re-sewing earned her the switch across her hands.

Elisa was always hungry, but mealtimes were horrible. If she put an elbow on the table, that elbow felt the switch. If she scratched her knee, again she felt the switch. If she dropped or spilled anything, the rest of the meal was taken away. When she dared to complain, the governess's cruel scolding brought her to tears. Over and over, she was forced to recite an apology:

"Please forgive me. I'm a foolish girl who must learn better manners. I promise never to speak out of turn, again."

Elisa could read very well, but could not tell Kimball how she had learned. She remembered following the words when her aunt read her *Pride and Prejudice*. By the time she was four, Elisa had been reading on her own. Kimball allowed her full range of the old but ample house library. Elisa was pleased, until the governess, bored during long dark evenings, insisted that Elisa read aloud to entertain her. Reading aloud meant lessons in elocution with punishment for mistakes. Elisa had a quick ear, so her thick Yorkshire dialect soon smoothed into acceptable upper class English.

Constant berating slowly wore down Elisa's spirit. During the first days, she asked to go outside. Since there was no manicured garden Kimball felt was appropriate for a young lady to take exercise, Elisa was forced to stay indoors. When she reasonably suggested that exercise was healthful, Kimball placed a book on her head, ordering her to cross the room a hundred times. Each time the book fell, ten crossings were added. Many nights Elisa fell asleep exhausted, frustrated, and totally miserable.

Five months passed and Sir John Garingham's return approached. Kimball became even stricter. She had been promised a bonus if Elisa behaved like a lady, and was determined to earn it. Knowing he would look at Elisa's hands, she massaged her fingers with lanolin. Her nails and cuticles had healed and grown out evenly. Caning her palms sometimes left them red and swollen. Now, every time the girl committed an offense, a mark was made on the chalkboard. At the end of the day, when she was in her nightdress, that many strokes stabbed the backs of her thighs.

Elisa had no idea who Sir John Garingham was, or why everyone was so afraid of him. Every time she asked, she was told it was none of her concern. Since he had turned her life from heaven into hell, she felt it was very much her concern.

One night, shortly before his return, she lay in bed with throbbing legs, trying to understand. Why was this happening to her? What had she done wrong? Was she going to be thrashed every night for the rest of her life? She sobbed into her pillow. Whoever Sir John was, he wanted her to be a lady. That was why he sent for a governess. If Elisa pleased him, perhaps he would send Kimball away.

Yes! That must be it. A surge of hope set her tender heart racing. Perhaps he'll bring Pony Billy back. Elisa decided to do her very best. If Sir John was pleased, all would be well again. For the first time in weeks, she curled up happily and fell asleep.

*

Tea with Sir John Garingham was a complete success. Dressed in an expensive new frock, pristine high-button shoes, her hair in soft lustrous curls, Elisa looked like a beautiful Dresden doll. She behaved perfectly. She smiled, kept her eyes demurely low, spoke only when spoken too, used all the correct utensils, sat like a lady, and spilled nothing. She had composed a poem, written it out with exact copperplate strokes, and embroidered a handkerchief. Sir John nodded with stern approval and slipped Miss Kimball an envelope. Anthony Roundtree and his sister sighed with relief as they escorted him to the door.

Elisa waited breathlessly for word of her reprieve. Instead, she heard Kimball's voice. "Back to the nursery, Miss Elisa. We have lessons to finish."

Elisa froze. This could not be true.

Kimball glared. "Well? What are you waiting for?"

"But, I did well." The little girl boldly stood her ground. "I behaved like a lady. Now he'll send you away."

Kimball's lips spread into a smirk. "Is that what you thought? If you did well, my job would be done?" She laughed in a way that made Elisa shudder. "You stupid child. This was a test to insure my permanent employment. I am here to stay."

"No!" Elisa flew upstairs to her room, slamming the door behind her. Too late, she remembered that the key was on the outside. Kimball's footsteps sounded on the stairs. Knowing there was no other escape, Elisa threw open a window, hiked up her skirt, and climbed onto the trellis. The fabric caught on the thorny rose canes. Violently pulling away, she ripped the expensive needlework.

Kimball appeared at the window above her. "Come back here at once."

Elisa frantically tore the skirt, lost her footing, and fell to the ground.

Kimball screamed. "I'll give you the beating of your life."

Like a terrified doe, Elisa ran through the woods onto her beloved moors. She rushed blindly, without direction, until she collapsed, shivering, against a rock. A freezing rain started to fall, first gently then harder. She was miserably cold, but stayed where she was. Death would be a welcome relief.

*

When Elisa opened her eyes, every part of her body ached. A maid looked up from her darning. "Yer awake, then?"

Elisa tried to speak. Her tongue felt thick. Her limbs were too heavy to move.

The maid called down the stairs, "Miss Roundtree! Miss Elisa's awake."

Aunt Lillian scurried in. "Oh, dear child. How do you feel? You must try and eat something, today."

Elisa had been missing for two days before a shepherd found her on the moors, soaking wet and burning with fever. The doctor had been called and the fever broke within hours. He expected her to recover quickly. When she lingered, day after day, refusing food, and crying for no apparent reason, he feared she had lost her sanity. Every time Kimball came into the room, Elisa screamed and burst into tears.

Hiding in the hallway, Kimball watched the maid carry away Elisa's untouched luncheon tray. She glided to the bedside. "Not a sound!"

Elisa cowered under the covers.

"I have an arrangement to offer you."

Elisa's eyes opened wide.

"Sir John promised me a bonus, if I whipped you into shape, quickly."

At the word "whip," Elisa grimaced.

"I was very harsh with you, but it was accomplished. He was pleased. If he learns how ill you are now, he will be extremely displeased."

"Why does he care?"

"I have no idea. You have no breeding, no pedigree. This estate is worth little, but that is none of my affair. What is my affair is my position in this house." Pursing her lips, she took a deep breath. "You are extremely intelligent. Anything you wish to learn, you learn quickly and well. Those things you do not wish to learn..." She rolled her eyes. "Well... here is my offer."

Elisa listened eagerly.

"I cannot promise never to cane you again...,"

"Then there's no arrangement." Although pale and thin, the girl had a will of iron.

Kimball was secretly impressed. "Very well. I will present what you must learn in order to become a lady. I will not allow sloth, but you may learn at your own pace."

"May I go outside?"

"There is no suitable place..." The girl glared, and the governess clenched her jaw. "Yes."

"Every day?"

"Weather permitting, every day."

*

Throughout his daughter's illness, Anthony Roundtree had been frantic. To keep her from running away again, he nailed her two large windows closed. A small side window was allowed to open for fresh air. A stronger lock was put on the outside of her door. He never visited her or asked how she was feeling. He was only frightened that she might die. Once she was out of danger, he seemed to forget she existed.

Kimball was true to her word. The cane vanished. Her ridiculing tongue became a cruel substitute, often reducing Elisa to tears. When Elisa dared to defend herself, she was denied food. Every afternoon, before tea, Elisa ran outside, breathing the sweet air of her Yorkshire Moors. She never felt the exhilaration of riding her pony, but having been a prisoner in her room, she never complained.

Warm weather arrived and Elisa's room became stifling. Her father refused to remove the nails and open the windows. That, plus the isolation of the estate, drove Kimball to seek employment elsewhere. Elisa was thrilled when she left. Other governesses came and went, but Elisa controlled them all. She had a dozen hiding places filled with books and candle stubs. Entire days flew by with a stash of bread and cheese and a good book. Now, if Elisa was sent to bed without supper, the servants slipped her food, or let her out at night then locked her back in, before morning.

Twice a week, a music mistress from the village taught Elisa to sing and play the piano. The woman was kind and an excellent musician. Elisa loved the lessons and learned quickly. After only a few months, she was entertaining her aunt and their infrequent guests. Her father and Sir John Garingham recognized that young ladies should be musical. Since neither had any appreciation, after a few bars, they either resumed their conversation, or left the room.

Chapter Eleven

November 1897

Sir John Garingham rarely came to call. When he did, Elisa stayed out of sight. Often, he had no desire to see her, and she was always relieved when his motorcar drove away. Today she sat in her windowsill, looking down into the yard, watching his chauffeur polish the shiny black metal and silver chrome on his expensive motorcar. The day was cold and bright, and she longed to be outside. Past experience had taught her patience. She would hide until Sir John called for her. It was past the noon dinner hour and she was hungry. Hunger pains were preferable to the torment of sitting at the table, remembering her perfect manners, and pretending to be pleased by Sir John's company.

There was a soft knock on her open door. A young maid stood on the threshold. "Pardon Miss Elisa, but you and Miss Lillian are wanted 't dinner." Usually fresh faced and cheerful, the girl's eyes were red from crying. Her hair and clothes were neat, but her face was pale. Her fingers shook, and her voice was faint.

Elisa stared at the maid. "Whatever is the matter, Annie? Are you ill?"

Annie stood tall and stared straight ahead. "Nowt's wrong, Miss. A'm raight as rain." She sniffed, "Please come, Miss. Master's waitin'." This sounded like a desperate plea and Elisa leapt from her perch.

"Of course."

Elisa watched Annie hurry away toward Lillian's rooms. She was limping in pain.

When Elisa arrived downstairs, Sir John was chuckling happily and sipping sherry with her father. Elisa was pleased his mood was good, but wondered why. He looked Elisa up and down, smiling with yellow teeth. Her father looked at her, then at Sir John. Both men laughed in a way that made Elisa cringe. She lowered her eyes and said nothing.

Sir John turned to Roundtree, "Well, I've worked up an appetite." He looked around, "Where's that giddy sister of yours?"

Lillian scurried down the stairs looking white as a ghost. She silently nodded to the men, and led the way into dinner.

The meal was as Elisa expected. The men seemed to forget ladies were at the table. Since Elisa was never addressed, she never spoke. Her aunt usually dared interject a few comments which were either ignored or snubbed. Today, she was also silent. Elisa guessed it had something to do with Annie.

Elisa was ravenous, but cut socially acceptable tiny bites of food, and tried to ignore both men, laughing so raucously food fell from their mouths. Roundtree's hair and moustache were cut short, but Sir John's hair was long. Greasy strands stuck to his sideburns.

Pudding was served, and the ladies were finally able to excuse themselves. Before they could leave, Sir John spoke to Lillian. "That girl Annie, I have a button for her to sew. Send her to me in the guest bedroom, in a half-hour." He turned away, as a footman offered a box of cigars.

Lillian spoke for the first time. "Annie is ill. I have sent her to bed."

Both Sir John and Roundtree stared daggers at her. Elisa knew something terrible was happening, but had no idea what. She watched Sir John choose a cigar. His former good humor was gone.

He practically growled, "Then *you* will have to sew the button." He pointed with the cigar. "Half - an - hour."

Tears filled Lillian's eyes. "Yes, Sir John. Half-an-hour." She sped upstairs.

Elisa hurried to follow, but Roundtree called her back, "Elisa."

She stopped, whispering, "Yes, Father?" She lowered her eyes.

"Go take one of your walks. Stay away for an hour."

Sir John slightly shook his head and Roundtree corrected himself. "Stay away for two hours." He pointed a finger. "Do you hear?"

Elisa was frightened. "Yes sir. Two hours." She curtsied, raced for her coat and hat, and hurried outside, through the narrow woods and onto the bright moors. She marched for a quarter hour before she stopped and rested on a rock. Watching contented sheep graze on the scarce grass and thorny bushes, she wondered why she had been sent away. Was Annie really ill? Why was Lillian afraid to sew on a button, and why did both men want her out of the house?

When Elisa returned, Sir John's motorcar was gone. She sighed with relief. Her walk had been so pleasant, and she was so tired, she forgot she had been sent outside. Now, slowly approaching the house, she became fearful. Was Annie truly ill? Had anything happened when Aunt Lillian sewed Sir John's button?

She hung up her coat and listened. There was no sound. Usually her aunt chatted as the servants prepared tea. Elisa was hungry again, but there were no familiar sounds of cutlery and dishes being set. The house was eerily silent. She hurried to her aunt's bedroom. The door was open. She was surprised to see Lillian's maid bathing her aunt's face with a cool cloth. A bruise was forming across her eye and cheek.

Elisa was horrified. "Auntie, what's happened?"

Lillian started to cry, and the maid soothed her. "There, there, now Miss Lillian." She smiled at Elisa. "Yer auntie's taken a fall, 'tis all. She'll have a nasty bruise for a week or so. Then, tha' won't even know 'tis happened."

Lillian clasped her knees together and sobbed into her pillow.

The maid blinked back tears. "Miss Elisa, y'd best get yer tea below stairs w' t' servants. I know y' dan mind."

Elisa backed away. "Of course I don't mind." She hurried downstairs.

The other servants sat around the table whispering angrily. They saw Elisa and stopped. She was frantic. "What's happened? Please tell me. First Annie took ill, now Auntie's had this fall…,"

The cook coughed a laugh. "Fall is it? That's what they told y'?"

Elisa sat down beside her. "Please tell me…,"

All the servants shared a look and shook their heads. The cook patted Elisa's hand. "Nowt t' worry. Sir John Garingham's nowt be back fer a long time. Tha's all tha need to know."

Chapter Twelve

December 1899

Sir John Garingham stayed away for two years. His unwelcome return coincided with Elisa's fourteenth birthday. Her Aunt Lillian planned a party. Sir John sent Elisa a new frock with matching slippers, stockings, gloves and, for the first time, a corset. Elisa had grown several inches that year, and was very thin.

"I had hoped the discomfort of a corset could wait until you were older," Aunt Lillian said, "But...,"

When the whalebone harness was pulled from its box, Elisa shuddered. "Is this more of the misery of womanhood?"

Her aunt smiled and weakly nodded. A few weeks before, Elisa had woken in the night with fierce pain in her stomach. Blood seeped between her legs. She thought she was dying.

"Women suffer, child. Now you know. The pain and blood will come every month, for the rest of your life," her aunt had told her.

Since no further explanation was given, she thought womanhood was a curse.

When Elisa was dressed in the new ensemble, Aunt Lillian started to cry. Elisa was only aware that she could not breathe. Her head felt light and she thought she would faint. She managed to gasp short breaths. "Whatever is the matter now, Aunt? Don't I look well?"

Her Aunt wiped away her tears. "You look beautiful, Elisa. You look like a woman, so much like your...," Lillian ran from the room weeping. Elisa and the housemaid shared a sad head shake, watching the sweet demented lady go.

The maid puffed Elisa's sleeves and made finishing touches to her hair. Very carefully, Elisa took short breaths and walked downstairs to greet her guests. Young girls from the village church giggled as Elisa showed off her new womanly shape.

Her father and Sir John smoked cigars and watched the silly girls from an adjoining room.

Roundtree smiled. "She's growing up, Sir John."

"Indeed she is. She's lovely."

"Worth the wait?"

"She'd be worth it if she were ugly as Beelzebub." Sir John's eyes lingered on her budding young breasts, pushing against the soft fabric. Letting his glance play down across her impossibly tiny waist, he took in her slender hips, wondering if soft red hairs were sprouting between her legs.

Roundtree guessed his friend's fantasy. "You don't have to wait 'til she's eighteen. That factory merger, last week? The owner's daughter was sixteen."

"I read about it. Her father arranged it."

"Well?" Roundtree swaggered.

Sir John raised an eyebrow. "I've invested this much and waited this long. I'm not going to do something stupid and ruin it all. I don't need some German relative turning up, challenging my claim to her estate. Also, I need her mature enough to give me healthy sons. I don't want her dying, like her mother. I won't feel really secure until I have two sons to inherit."

A pretty maid carried in a tray of food.

Sir John looked her up and down. "What's her name?"

"Agnes."

"Have you had her yet?"

"She's new. Gave me the run around."

Sir John smiled. "Good. I like women who are very willing or very unwilling. Otherwise it's no fun. What happened to Annie? I liked her."

"Got in trouble. I chucked her out."

"Too bad. She fought like a tiger." Garingham puffed casually on his cigar. "Gone to the workhouse?"

Roundtree shrugged. "Who knows where these girls go. Couldn't give her a reference, in her condition."

After tea, the guests played hide and seek. Elisa hid in the pantry. Sir John followed her. Hearing footsteps, she turned, laughing, expecting a girlfriend. Sir John leered over her, backing her into a corner. He had not touched her since that morning, years ago, when he dragged her away from Pony Billy's cart. Now, his hands reached around her waist. His fingers squeezed the whalebone. "How slim you are. I can reach my fingers all the way around."

Elisa lurched against the wall. "It's the corset, sir. I've never worn one before."

He pushed his knee between her legs. One hand held her arm like a vice while the other slipped over her breast. His mouth pressed against hers. Struggling to get away, she felt his tongue push against her pursed lips.

A girl's voice called, "Elisa! Game's over. Sally's turn."

Startled, Sir John stood back.

Elisa flew past him and sped upstairs to her aunt's room. When she calmed enough to explain what happened, Lillian sadly shook her head. "He's your betrothed, dearest. He has the right."

Elisa was appalled. "What do you mean, he's my betrothed?"

Her aunt wrung her hands. "He is a very wealthy man. He has been supporting us since before you were born."

Elisa grabbed the bedstead for support.

Lillian wrung her hands. "We have nothing. Nothing at all. I've told you about darling Charlie, our blessed older brother."

She walked to a large family portrait that hung over the hearth. Elisa knew she was about to hear an old story. Lillian's father and mother sat in front of four children. Charlie and Lillian, half-grown, were slender and redheaded, like Elisa. Their younger brother Anthony had dark hair. The smallest child and a baby in her mother's arms had died and were never spoken of.

Lillian smiled and pointed to her elder brother. "Charlie was very clever with money. If he had lived, all would be well. He was an engineer, working on the Suez Canal. After he was killed in an accident, Tony inherited. He gambled, then drove the estate to ruin. Now, the farm earns almost nothing. I had no dowry. I could never marry and had to stay here. My darling, you also have no dowry. If it weren't for Sir John Garingham, we might be in the poorhouse. We owe him everything."

Not believing any of it, Elisa waited until the guests had gone and braved asking her father. He was annoyed. "Of course, you stupid girl. Why do you think he's spending so much money on your education? You're going to school in the fall. You'll stay there for four years, then you'll marry him."

Chapter Thirteen

Oxford, September 1901

Rory Cookingham bent over his study desk, meticulously copying the last sentences of his fifty-five page paper on the *1861 Offense Against Young Persons Act*. He carefully dotted the last period. *Perfect*! He stretched, rubbed his sore eyes, stared in a mirror, and shuddered. He was nineteen, short and blond, and looked like an exhausted schoolboy.

He moved back to his desk and carefully proofread the page. "...*after lengthy consideration for*..." He tensed. That should have been, "...*lengthy consideration of*..." He would have to rewrite the entire page. Was it worth it? He clenched his jaw, *Yes*! He crumpled the otherwise perfect page, tossed it into his overflowing trash basket and began copying the perfect letters, again.

At four-thirty that afternoon, bathed, shaved, and dressed in a beautifully tailored suit, Rory tied a neat ribbon around his pristine academic paper. The cover, and each of the fifty-five pages, looked like they had been professionally copied. Every margin was perfect. Exactly the same number of lines was on each page, and there was not one single ink smudge, anywhere.

Very happy, he tucked the manuscript under one arm, took his small traveling bag, and walked outside double-quick.

Rory's tutor, Frederick Brown, was past middle-aged, short and round. Rory had never seen him without smudged spectacles and a soiled academic gown tossed over a frayed suit.

"Ah, Cookingham! What bit of entertaining perspicacity have you brought me today?" The tutor's eyes sparkled as he took the manuscript and read the first lines. "Capital! This will be my evening's read. If only the rest of your class was up to your speed. We spoke about your accelerating. Anytime you like, I'll speak to the dean."

"Thank you, sir, but I'm in no hurry to leave Oxford."

"Really? I would have thought...,"

"To be honest, sir, once I leave these ivy covered walls, I'll have to accept a tedious position, sit at a solicitor's desk ten-hours-a-day, six-days-a-week, for a starting wage smaller than my current allowance. Completing my assignments early allows me free time I may never enjoy again, for the rest of my life, so I am in no hurry to earn my degree."

"Ah, that puts the situation in a new light. You can easily continue your studies and become a teacher."

Rory grimaced. "Again, sir, with all due respect, the celibate life accompanying the profession…,"

"…definitely has its shortcomings." Brown laughed.

"Also, sir, my whole life, I've been accelerated beyond my age level. It was fine, when I was a boy. Now, I dread growing up."

"How old are you, Cookingham?"

"Nineteen, sir. I won't be twenty until June."

"With the plan I had in mind, you would have been one of the youngest students to degree, ever. You could easily continue. Eventually go for the silk."

He smiled sadly. "I'd love to become a barrister, but I'm a third son. My father won't pay for me to study any longer than necessary."

"Pity." Brown saw Rory's traveling bag. "Off for a week end?"

"Yes sir. To visit my aunt."

"Really?" He winked and whispered. "Well, I hope your aunt is twenty, pretty and willing."

Rory choked on a laugh.

"Well, off you go then."

At seven-thirty, Rory escorted a saucy shop girl toward the huge white stone pillars framing the ornately carved entrance to His Majesty's Theatre. Rory and his young lady were not dressed in formal eveningwear, so he bought tickets high up in the gallery. Even there, the seats were plush red velvet, the banisters polished, and the trimmings glistening gold.

The curtain rose and he was entranced. An Italian city spread before him and richly clothed citizens went about their business. After chuckling at the silly opening, he was quickly involved in the story. When Katherine Stewart entered as Kate, he stopped breathing. She was the most beautiful woman he had ever seen. Her shrew was ferocious, but vulnerable. Every expression, every subtle inflection of her voice wrenched his heart.

Jeremy O'Connell entered as Petruchio and Rory felt himself pushed back in his chair. He had never felt such power exude from a man. When Jeremy and Katherine were on stage together, the walls stretched to contain their energy. They were certainly in love. No one could pretend that kind of passion.

For days after, Rory thought only of the world on stage at His Majesty's Theatre. With no social connections in London, he could not meet upper-class young ladies. Deciding solitude was preferable to the company of uneducated shop girls, he returned alone, week-after-week, to see Jeremy O'Connell as *Ulysses*, *Volpone*, and the Captain of *H.M.S. Pinafore*. O'Connell could even sing.

Every time Rory saw a play, he hurried back to Oxford and borrowed a copy from the college library. His fascination grew. How did O'Connell harness his passions, his rage? How did he cry on cue? How did all the actors create life from dry words?

Ready to explode with questions, he made a bold move. He wrote Jeremy O'Connell a letter.

Chapter Fourteen

London, December 1901

During the reign of Queen Victoria, the great actor-manager Herbert Beerbohm Tree built Her Majesty's Theatre. King Edward was crowned in 1901, and the name became His Majesty's Theatre. When Tree took his acting company on an American tour, Eric Bates's penny-pinching wife Hilda saw an opportunity to make money, and leased the magnificent theatre.

Blissfully, if temporarily performing on that glorious stage, Jeremy and Katherine became gigantic stars, drawing large salaries as well as a percentage of the ticket sales. "O'Connell and Stewart" become household names, and audiences thrilled to see a happily married couple revealing their love, playing theatrical characters.

At thirty-nine, Jeremy O'Connell was handsome, strong, and the happiest of men.

He had even grown to like Eric Bates. Although Eric had little imagination, under Jeremy's direction, he became an excellent character actor. Hilda Bates brilliantly handled the finances, allowing Jeremy freedom to manage everything artistic.

Shortly before Katherine's son Evan was born, Jeremy moved them into two wonderful flats, one above the other, in a fashionable part of town. Each flat contained a large drawing-room and master bedroom, a guestroom, a study, kitchen and servants' quarters. Katherine's flat was upstairs, Jeremy's was below, and Evan had a room in each. There was a staircase running between the floors, with doors at the top and bottom. Simply by closing the door on their floor, they insured privacy.

Simon Camden dashed into town every couple of years and bedded down with Katherine. Other than that, she happily nurtured now eight-year-old Evan, lived like a nun, and frequently cuddled with Jeremy in his large downstairs bed.

From the first, Evan was a sensitive, precocious child, and the delight of Jeremy's life. Strikingly handsome, blond and blue-eyed like his mother, Evan was an exact miniature of her. He looked as much like Jeremy as Eric. As far as their adoring audiences knew, Katherine and Jeremy were happily married, and Evan was their child. Their bohemian community included every vareity of family unit. From birth, Evan had been told the his "Uncle Eric" was his real father, and Eric's daughters his half sisters. Evan was a very happy child, adored onstage and off. He appeared in every possible boy's role and was becoming a fine actor.

One afternoon, Jeremy settled behind the kidney-shaped desk in his office, reviewing a pile of fan letters. Most, he skimmed and tossed into a bin. He and Katherine kept the secretary supplied with pre-autographed note cards. He skimmed one letter, stopped, checked the signature, and carefully reread it from the top. A chap named Rory Cookingham asked about Petruchio in *Taming Of The Shrew*.

"Why did Shakespeare write Petruchio's excellent speeches in fine, upper-class prose, then bequeath him the personality of a slovenly lout?"

Jeremy cringed. He had made Petrucio a slovenly lout because it made audiences laugh. It was his choice, not Shakespeare's. Obviously, it had not made Rory laugh.

The next observation was easier to counter.

"Kate and Petrichio fall so honestly in love, I think it is only possible for a married couple, like you and Miss Stewart, to play those roles to perfection."

Smirking to himself, Jeremy lied, writing that he had toured with two different actresses playing Kate, and their love scenes appeared equally real to their audiences.

Rory continued with:

"The next week, I was amazed to see Miss Stewart, as The Duchess Of Malfi, fall in love, equally convincingly, with a dissimilar actor. I understand that acting upon the stage is just that, but I am also curious. Most men would not willingly place their wives into the arms of other men..."

Jeremy winced again. *The Duchess Of Malfi* was the tragic love story of an older woman and a younger man. At thirty-four, Katherine was blossoming into middle-age. The twenty-five-year-old actor Jeremy cast opposite her was a striking black-Irishman called Owen Freeman. A

72

pompous ass off-stage, Owen was a fine actor and their on-stage chemistry was electric. Believing Katherine was long overdue some manly attention, Jeremy engineered Owen into her bed. Since she did not really like him, she was well serviced, without the risk of falling in love and leaving Jeremy.

Cookingham's final questions were about historical and geographic inaccuracies, and outright mistakes in Jeremy's translation from the Greek in *Ulysses*. Jeremy answered these questions without much consideration, and days later received another letter, questioning his hasty answers. Simultaneously annoyed and thrilled that someone actually cared, and was clever enough to challenge him, a long dormant spark of intellectual curiosity set Jeremy's brain ablaze.

That letter was followed by another, then another. Each time this remarkable scholar asked difficult questions and made astute observations that forced Jeremy to restudy topics he took for granted.

One afternoon, Jeremy and his valet Max dragged boxes from a storage closet. Jeremy emptied a crate, and ancient leather bindings crashed to the floor. Jeremy searched through ancient textbooks like a squirrel hunting for a nut.

Evan dove onto the floor beside him. Dust blew up and the boy rubbed his blue eyes. "What are you looking for, Daddy? Can I help?"

"My Greek dictionary. I haven't used it since university, but it should be here somewhere"

Max coughed. "Could this be it?" He held up a much worn, dark green volume.

Jeremy took it quickly. "Yes. Excellent." He sped to his study and paged through the dictionary. Rory's letter lay on the blotter.

Evan was close on his heels. "Can I see?"

Jeremy stretched his arm so Evan could climb into his lap, pulled the letter closer, and compared the handwritten Greek on the stationary to the printed Greek in the dictionary.

Evan strained to see the comparison. "What does it say?"

Jeremy sighed. "It says that Ulysses traveled *over* the water. In my staging, Ulysses swims the river. Since the correct translation is 'over' and not 'through,' Ulysses could not possibly swim 'over' the water. He must have taken a boat or a raft of some sort. My staging is nonsense."

Evan studied the odd pen marks. "But you told me that *Ulysses* wasn't a true story."

"That is correct. It is a myth."

"Then, what does it matter, if the translation is wrong? It's all made up, anyway."

Jeremy chuckled and kissed the soft platinum-blond hair on top of his head. "That is something your mother would say. And you are correct. Still, it bothers me. If this Oxford chap noticed the inaccuracy, others may have as well. He has listed two other mistakes in the translation. I have no doubt that he is correct."

Evan read the name at the bottom of the letter. "Rory Cook-ing-ham. What a funny name."

"It is, rather. But the chap is very clever. I look forward to his letters. His questions keep me on my toes."

"He's not as clever as you are. You're the smartest man in the entire world."

Pleased by the boy's blind adoration, Jeremy chortled and gave him a squeeze. "Thank you, darling, but I am not the smartest man in the world, not by a long shot."

"But you are. You know everything."

"I did not know that Ulysses traveled *over* the water." Evan's narrow shoulders heaved unhappily, and Jeremy laughed. "I am sorry, but there are a great many scholars, statesmen and clergymen who know more than I do. Of course only God knows everything." Evan looked upset and Jeremy felt lost. "I am *possibly* the greatest actor in the world. It is also *possible* that my productions are the best in the world. Of course, your Uncle Simon would argue both of those suppositions."

Evan whispered, "You're the best father in the world. Even if you're not my real father." He put his thin arms around Jeremy's neck. They held each other tight.

"That one I will accept. Thank you."

Evan looked back at the letter. "Mr. Cookingham must be very clever."

"Indeed. He is."

Oxford

"Cooky! You've got mail!"

74

"Thanks, Plunky." Rory took three envelopes from his friend and started upstairs. The first was a letter from his mother and the next from his eldest brother. The postmark on the third read: *London / Haymarket / His Majesty's Theatre*. His palms were moist as he carefully broke the seal. With a pounding heart, he read bold words, written in the florid hand of Jeremy O'Connell.

Never expecting a response to his letter, Rory was thrilled to receive four pages of detailed answers to his questions, as well as Jeremy's personal philosophies on literary and historical points. In his research, Rory discovered that the original 1594 title was *THE TAMING OF A SHREW*. Jeremy wrote back, saying that was an entirely different play, possibly written by a different playwright, nearly thirty years before Shakespeare's 1623 play, *THE TAMING OF THE SHREW*. This sent Rory back to the library, where he discovered the character of "Petruchio" in still another, 1597 play, *THE TAMER TAMED*. Each question was answered and each answer raised another question.

Chapter Fifteen

May 1902

HIS MAJESTY'S THEATRE
TODAY AT 3:00
Mr. JEREMY O'CONNELL
Miss KATHERINE STEWART
FINAL PERFORMANCE of THE TAMING OF THE SHREW

Today was extraordinary for two reasons:

First, the final curtain fell on the final performance of an almost sold out run of Jeremy's third production of *The Taming Of The Shrew*.

Second, Jeremy was finally going to meet Rory Cookingham. After weeks of corresponding, Jeremy had invited Rory to tea.

Jeremy sat in his dressing gown, removing his makeup, wondering if Rory was as nervous as he was. A portion of the hall reflected in his mirror, and a short blond boy stood waiting in the corridor. No one else was in sight.

A few minutes later, he checked the reflection again. The boy was still there. No -- it couldn't be. The boy nervously wiped his upper lip and pushed thick blond hair off his forehead. Jeremy stared at the reflection. "Mr. Cookingham?"

"Yes, sir." The boy stood to attention.

"Do come in." Could that scholar's mind be lodged inside this boy's body?

"Thank you, sir."

Rory Cookingham walked into Jeremy's dressing room and smiled. An oriental rug covered the floor and green velvet drapes swayed against the partially opened window. He looked over Jeremy's carved wooden furniture, polished stove, exquisite china tea set, gilt mirrors, framed photos and letters. Symmetrically hung clothing, an immaculate dressing table with perfect rows of grease sticks, charcoal pencils, and fake hair for moustaches and beards completed this tiny jewel of a room.

A nervous laugh escaped his throat. "Forgive me, sir, but I think I've just walked through the looking glass."

After a few casual pleasantries, Jeremy finished dressing. Rory followed him from the theatre and across the street to the Red Lion Pub. Jeremy pushed open wide stained-glass and mahogany doors that led into a large L-shaped room. The floors and some of the walls were paneled in the same dark wood. Red flocking covered other walls and red cloths covered the tables. Padded leather chairs stood around each table, and booths with leather benches stood against the walls. Huge carved mirrors, paintings, and signed photographs of theatrical and musical personalities warmed the pub's elegant atmosphere. Wonderful smells poured from the kitchen.

When Jeremy and Rory walked up to the bar, a slight man with a huge gray beard nodded from behind the polished counter. "Afternoon Mr. O'Connell, Sir. Wha' can I getcha both?"

Pretending to watch the barman pour their drinks, Jeremy inventoried the young scholar. It never occurred to him that Rory could be short. He was only slightly taller than Katherine. He looked very fit. His suit was cut from soft, expensive wool, his collar was new, his tie immaculate, and his thick, fair hair beautifully cut. They took their drinks, then moved to the back, through a room full of theatre patrons. Jeremy led Rory to a corner booth, where they could have privacy.

The second they were seated, Rory's question bubbled out. "Please, sir, was it my imagination, or were you and Miss Stewart different, today? I mean, in my letter I asked…"

"I remember what you asked. I also remember that I chose not to answer the question."

Rory's heart pounded. "I beg your pardon, sir. I hope I didn't offend."

Jeremy stifled a smile. "When one party is correct, offense is usually given to the other party, who is usually incorrect. In this case, Mr. Cookingham, *you* were correct.

Rory chuckled and Jeremy smiled back.

A waitress carried over their dinners, and Rory dove his fork into a steaming steak and ale pie. Jeremy elegantly de-boned half a chicken. They ate in silence for a few minutes.

"Mr. Cookingham?"

"Yes, sir." He answered with his mouth full.

"How old are you?"

Nearly spitting out his food, Rory wiped his mouth with his serviette. "Nineteen sir. I was pushed ahead in school."

"Pushed ahead? I dare say you flew. Of course, if your letters are any example of your spoken dialogue, your relentless questions must drive your masters mad."

Rory chuckled nervously. "You are correct, sir. It was like that at school. At university, it is quite the opposite. They chide the lads who don't ask questions. And most don't. I had thought that Oxford chaps would all be brilliant." Jeremy smiled, so Rory plowed ahead. "I am so grateful you answered my letters. You taught me so much. I had seen lots of plays, but it never occurred to me that an actor could be... um...,"

"Could be a scholar?"

"Yes sir."

Jeremy leaned back, half-closing his eyes. "I have enjoyed your letters. More than I can say. I am not used to being challenged. Now, I wish that you had seen '*Shrew*,' and given me your critique a year ago. You noticed I had lost the wonder of seeing Kate for the first time." He shook his head. "Living with a beautiful woman... you can take her for granted. Never mind. It is time we put '*The Shrew*' to bed. We have been playing her for years and we have gotten very stale."

"But, how did you do it, sir? Today..." He stared up with large blue eyes. "How did you find that 'wonder'?"

He was adorable, but not a pouf. Jeremy crossed his arms to keep his hands from doing something embarrassing. "Regaining wonder, Mr. Cookingham, or any feeling, is an actor's job, an actor's technique. In its simplest form, it is replaying memory."

Rory took a moment to digest the phrase. "'Replaying... memory'?" He spoke slowly, visualizing his words. "When I 'replay' the phonograph, I hear the same music a second time. The music is imprinted on the cylinder."

Jeremy smiled. I love the way this boy thinks.

Rory concentrated. "Once words are printed on a page, they remain unchanged forever. Music can be replayed from manuscript." He looked at Jeremy. "But memory, sir? It is certainly imprinted, but can it be, replayed?"

Jeremy leaned forward. "What is a memory? Nothing more than a catalogue of feelings and sensations, sights, sounds, smells. What are you feeling right now?"

Rory coughed and wiped his hands.

"We both know that you are feeling nervous as a cat, but how are those nerves manifest?" He stared blankly, so Jeremy gestured to the soiled serviette he was clutching.

He let go of the cloth and looked at his hands. "My palms are sweating, and I gulped my food like a pig."

Jeremy chuckled. "Not quite like a pig, but that is a good start. How else is your body reacting?"

Rory rolled his shoulders. "My neck's like a block." He rubbed it. "I'm sweating there, too, and from my forehead."

"Good."

He concentrated. "My stomach's in a knot, and I don't think I've taken a breath for the last hour."

Jeremy laughed loudly. "Good. Very good. Now, should you ever need to play a scene where you were meeting someone terrifying, you can remember those feelings and replay them."

"Now I'm blushing, as well." He ran his fingers through his hair. "But how do I remember these feelings? How do I, replay them?"

"Practice m' boy. Acting technique, like any other technique, takes practice. And, I would give you exercises, if you were an actor, in my class." Jeremy tossed his serviette on the table and stood up. "It seems a pleasant evening and I believe you have some time before your train. Shall we walk?"

"Yes, sir, please. I'll fetch the coats." Rory hurried across the room.

Jeremy sighed, shaking his head. Rory Cookingham was a remarkable young man. He worshiped Jeremy, for the moment. Soon enough, he would discover Jeremy's secret life, feel betrayed, and hate him. It had happened before. Jeremy decided to send Rory on his way. When the young man returned with the coats and smiled with guileless adoration, Jeremy's resolve evaporated. He would never be able to send Rory on his way.

Outside the pub they were stopped by the piping voice of young Evan. Running at full tilt, the boy's white-blond hair blew back. "Daddy!" he stopped and panted, "Mummy's looking for you."

79

Jeremy put his hand on Evan's head. "Mr. Cookingham, allow me to present Master O'Connell. Master O'Connell, Mr. Cookingham."

Rory shook Evan's small hand. "I enjoyed your performance in *Ulysses*."

"Thank you, Mr. Cookingam. I read your letter about the Greek being wrong. Daddy looked up the words in the dictionary. He said that…,"

"Jerry darling, please…," Katherine walked up briskly. "I must have an answer, just a simple yes, or no." Rory saw Katherine and looked as if he were in love.

Jeremy rolled his eyes. "Oh bother, Katie! I suppose I must go."

"No! You must not. I am perfectly capable of going alone, but I must respond tonight."

"Miss Stewart, may I present Rory Cookingham, from Oxford."

She smiled and extended her hand. "How-do-you-do Mr. Cookingham. Jerry's so enjoyed your letters. Do keep them coming."

Rory kissed her hand. "You are too kind, Miss Stewart. I have enjoyed your performances, very much."

"And, you are kind to say so."

*

Rory Cookingham entered the rehearsal room to audit Jeremy O'Connell's acting class. These sessions were private. Visitors were not allowed. Rory was a young, attractive stranger, so many sniggered that he must be, "Jerry's new lad."

Twenty assorted actors and actresses clowned, sulked, or studied scripts. Most were in their twenties and thirties. A few were past middle age. The few as young as Rory were shabbily dressed apprentices. Rory wore perfectly fitting, fine tailored clothes.

The room was large and bare with three rows of sturdy chairs set up as an audience. The varnished floor was swept clean, the walls and domed windows were immaculate. As the wall clock struck 1:00, the clip of Jeremy's sharp leather heels set everyone scurrying into chairs.

Jeremy marched into the room looking stunning in an immaculate gray suit. He spotted Rory at the back, glowered, then proceeded to a small writing table at the side of the front row. Rory's chin dropped and he looked appropriately embarrassed. Jeremy had not forbidden him to come. His last letter had said, "…*attending my class would be a waste of your valuable time*." Jerry sat down, crossed his legs, and read a list of scenes lying on the table. "I see we are to be force-fed another dose of *Julius Caesar*." He looked at an actor in the crowd. "Brave of you, Mr. Tanner."

The actor stammered, "I'... I've been working on it, sir. It's loads better. You'll like it today, that's sure."

Jeremy raised an eyebrow. "You waited until the end, last week, so you should go first this week, but I would rather start with anything else. I am sure you do not mind." He read further. "*Oedipus, Alchemist, Trelawny, Midsummer, Dolls' House -- Dolls House*? Miss Tate, however, were you able to pry that script away from Charles Carrington?"

"I shagged him."

The room exploded with laughter. Looking shocked and excited, Rory strained to see the young lady who had spoken. Jeremy looked down his elegant nose. "Very resourceful, Miss Tate." As he read further, his lips spread into a reluctant smile. "*As You Like It*, Miss McCarthy and Mr. Burns. Good. Let us start with that."

A woman's voice called, "Michael, set the chairs, will you. I've got to fix my trousers."

Rory looked up, as a striking, bird-like girl stepped out of the audience and unbuttoned her skirt. It slithered to the ground, revealing slender hips and legs bound tight in a pair of boy's trousers. Her eyes were painted huge and dark, her long black hair was tied back, and her cheeks were thin and pale. She was Peg McCarthy, seventeen, one of two female apprentices. Hilda Bates refused to give apprentices wages, so Peg lived by her wits... and more. She flashed Rory a blazing smile. He smiled back, then colored and crossed his legs.

Jeremy chuckled at the clever girl. She had instantly discovered that Rory had money and was absolutely not, "Jerry's new lad."

Trying not to stare at Peg, Rory concentrated on actor Michael Burns, putting out chairs to make a theatrical set. Michael was medium height and slender. He had a shock of red hair and dazzling green eyes. He called, "Y' ready, Peg?" She sauntered onto the stage area, enjoying the stares of a dozen men.

Jeremy's voice rang out. "Is this *As You Like It* or *Camille*?"

Instantly adjusting her posture and attitude, Peg transformed herself into a boy. She sat next to Michael and they looked like school chums.

Their scene was a boy lecturing a young man about love. They finished and sat nervously, watching Jeremy.

He put a finger over his lips and raised an eyebrow. "Mr. Burns, you toured for a long time."

"Yes, sir. Over five years."

"It shows." Jeremy glared at him. "In five short minutes you have choked us with every cheap trick, fake boyish pose and scene stealing prank in the repertoire." He threw up his hands. "Where the bloody hell was Orlando?" Michael stared at the floor. "What does he want in this scene?"

"He says, he's dying from lovesickness."

"So what does he want?"

Michael shrugged. "I suppose he wants Rosalind?"

"Of course he wants Rosalind. Good God man, haven't you ever been in love?"

Michael yelled back, "Yes, I have been in love, sir." Then whispered, "Too often." He put his head in his hands.

"You do not think you enjoy that pain and yet you have invited it more than once. Perhaps you do enjoy it?"

Michael looked horrified, and Jeremy sat back, shaking his head. "We all enjoy it, Mr. Burns. The human race cannot get enough of it. We even write plays about it so we can watch other people in that same pain. Orlando is in love with that pain. He says, '*I would not be cured.*' If you wish to play this part, you must invite the memory of that pain from your own experience." He waited as Michael took a deep breath, sat back, and stared at the floor.

Rory leaned forward. He felt sorry for Michael.

Jeremy turned to Peg. She concentrated, soaking in every word. "Miss McCarthy, if ever a young woman has cause for sorrow, it is Rosalind. In the blink of an eyelash, through no fault of her own, she is condemned to die, unless she forfeits her home, her loved ones, and her dream of marital bliss. She is desperate for Orlando to prove himself and somehow save her life. Her words may be light, but their consequence can be terribly severe."

Jeremy looked at Michael. "Mr. Burns, are you ready to go again?"

This time, the scene was very different. Rory was impressed.

Peg made sure Rory had a clear view when she seductively pulled her skirt back over her trousers.

Jeremy looked over the list of scenes. "Oh, come, Mr. Tanner, let us get it over with. Torture us with poor Cassius one last time."

A good-looking, powerfully built, middle-aged man took the floor. He began to recite and Rory strained to listen. Jeremy closed his eyes and rested his head in his hand. When he finished, Jeremy looked up sleepily. "Thank you Mr. Tanner." He studied the list. "Next can we...?"

"P'Please, sir." Tanner stammered, "That was better. I know it was."

"No, Mr. Tanner, it was not." He stayed where he was, so Jeremy commanded, "Sit down!" He studied his list. "Mr. Pierce and Miss Linford, may we please have *A Midsummer Night's Dream*."

Rory's mouth fell open. Jeremy could be cruel.

Tanner stayed where he was, glaring daggers at Jeremy. Two young actors moved to the stage area, ignoring Tanner. Finally, red-faced and seething, he skulked back to his chair.

Acting class ended at 4:30 sharp. Rory sat alone, digesting all he had seen and heard. Most of it had been fascinating, some funny, some horrible. He glanced up and saw Peg McCarthy in the doorway, smiling.

"Sorry," he sprang up. "I suppose I should to be out of here."

She sashayed in. "You can stay if you want. No one will be rehearsing this late."

He grabbed his coat and smiled nervously. "I've got to be going anyway. There's a 5:30 train."

"Where to?"

"Oxford. I'm a student, just down for the day."

"Is there a later train?"

"Um... yes, there are several, actually."

"Well then, wouldn't you like to buy a girl a cup of tea?"

"I would, very much. Sorry, I seem to have forgotten my manners. Your scene was wonderful, by the way. You're a very good actress."

She smiled seductively. "I'm learning. What's your name?"

"Rory Cookingham." He smiled and offered his hand. She took it and looked him up and down. His heart pounded and his knees felt weak.

"I'm Peg McCarthy." She cocked her head. "The Rory is all right, but he'll change the other."

"What other?"

"The Cook…"

"Cookingham?"

"Mr. Bates, the theatre manager, says actors have to have easy names, otherwise the public can't remember."

"Oh, I'm not an actor. I just wanted to watch the class." He laughed nervously and helped her with her tattered coat.

She smiled over her shoulder. "Mr. O'Connell never allows guests in class. I'm surprised he let you."

"He didn't exactly 'let' me. I just came. I think he's angry."

"I wouldn't worry. If he didn't want you here, he'd have thrown you out."

He put on his own coat, new and beautifully tailored.

Peg looked him over. "Come on, then." She smiled and started down the stairs.

Two hours later, Rory lay naked and gasping, sweating, and exquisitely satisfied on a pile of rough muslin used for making flats.

After a meal at the Red Lion Pub, Peg gave him a backstage tour, ending in a storage room. It was musty and warm and Peg had fashioned herself a bed. A single candle flame shed uneven light over the cluttered space. Rory stared at a cobweb on the ceiling. "You sleep here?"

"Sometimes. It's nicer than my boarding house."

He shook his head. "How can this be nicer than anywhere?" Enjoying the sight of her slight, shapely body, he saw tears run down her cheeks.

He sat up. "Oh, I'm so sorry!"

She chuckled, "Don't be daft. I brought you here. I wanted it."

He had never heard a girl admit that.

Much to his dismay, her tears continued, silently washing the charcoal from around her eyes. She wiped the black away with her fingers. "You pulled out. I never had a bloke do that."

He ran his hand over her white skin. "It's bad enough that I shagged you after an hour's acquaintance, without leaving you a lifetime souvenir."

"Most men don't care. You're a gentleman."

He lay back. "A gentleman wouldn't be here at all."

She giggled. "You're certainly not one of Jerry's lads."

"Jerry's lads?"

"That's what everyone was sniggering about, when you came in." She sat up. "You do know about Mr. O'Connell?"

"What about him?"

"That he's a..." He stared at her, and she nervously sat back. "Not that there's anything wrong with it. I don't know what you..., " she stammered, "You and he... some gents like to do both, and that's all right."

"Oh!" He coughed a laugh, and sat up. "So that's it. Of course. It's so obvious." He smiled at her. "No, I'm not... Don't worry." He lay back and gazed at the ceiling. "That's why he was so cool when we met. His letters were full of passion, then he found out I wasn't...,"

"You write letters to each other?"

"There've been dozens. His are brilliant. It was after writing letters that he invited me to meet him. He must have been disappointed that I wasn't... Is Evan, O'Connell's...?"

"He's Eric Bates's son, but no one speaks of it. She looked into Rory's eyes, very bright in the dim light, then leaned over and kissed him. "You didn't like the makeup, did you?"

"I'm not used to it. You look younger without it."

"That's why I wear it, to look older. How old are you?"

"Nineteen. How old are you?"

"Seventeen."

"You're only seventeen?"

"Ya," she giggled. "I'm not a real actress, just an apprentice, no wages."

"How do you live?"

"I get some meals at the boarding house. For the rest," she smiled self-consciously, "I do what I can."

*

"Rory luv." A soft whisper in his ear.

He lurched awake. The candle was nearly out. "What's the time?"

Goin' on 7:00. I go' a' carry costumes down from wardrobe. We go' a show tonigh'."

He grabbed his clothes. "There's an 8:30 train. I've got an exam tomorrow." He shook his head. "It'll be an all-night-study now."

She quickly dressed. "I'm sorry. You was so 'andsome sleepin', Oi din' wan'a wake y'."

He stopped. What did she say?

Alarmed, she took a deep breath and over-pronounced, "I – didn't – want – to – wake – you." She saw the startled look on Rory's face and clenched her fists in frustration. "I can' keep it up any more, talkin' proper. U'm nackered." He continued to stare and she started to cry. "I'm learnin' to talk proper. Miss Stewart's 'elpin' me, but I can' keep it up all the time." Her eyes pleaded for approval. "You 'ate the way I talk, dan y'?

His eyes bulged and he hurriedly laced a shoe. "For heaven's sake, it doesn't matter how a person talks."

She smiled gratefully. "Y' mean tha'?

"Of course." *Bloody hell*! The way a person talked was everything. She was a better actress than she knew. He tossed his tie around his neck and grabbed his coat. "I'll be off, then."

Peg's heart was breaking. "Will y'," she took a deep breath and spoke slowly. "Will – you – be – back – next – week, for class?" She swallowed, forcing back tears.

He looked at her. She was so tiny, and so unhappy. "I'd like to. I don't know if I can, or if Mr. O'Connell will let me." An uneasy laugh escaped him. "He might throw me out the next time."

Tears streamed down her cheeks.

"Please don't cry." He threw down his coat, took her in his arms, kissed her, and suddenly desired her all over again. He pushed her away. "I'll try to come back. I can't promise."

She smiled gratefully and wiped her eyes. He pulled two crowns from his pocket and put them in her hand. "In case I don't get back, take a friend to tea, on me." He smiled, took his coat, and ran out.

*

It was 7:15 when Jeremy next saw Rory Cookingham. He thought Rory had gone back to Oxford. When he appeared at the dressing-room door, Jeremy was in an easy chair, elegantly wrapped in a hand-painted silk dressing gown. He had a long-stemmed pipe in one hand and a book in the other.

"Still here, Mr. Cookingham?"

"Yes, sir." Rory stood awkwardly, waiting to be invited inside. His suit was rumpled and the ends of his hair were dark with sweat.

Enjoying the young man's discomfort, and wondering what vigorous pursuit had occupied his last three hours, Jeremy held his steady gaze, puffed on his pipe, and surrounded himself with sweet smoke.

Rory shifted nervously from one foot to the other. "Your class was wonderful, sir. Thank you so much for allowing me to watch."

"What was so wonderful?"

"Watching trained actors do the things you have taught me."

"Have I taught you?"

"Oh, yes sir. In a few letters and one supper, I have learned more from you than from two years at University. You have taught me to understand people, their feelings, desires, and struggles. At Oxford, I have learned nothing but meaningless legal precepts."

Jeremy allowed his lips to curve into a smile.

"There was one thing, sir. You were wrong about that line in OEDIPUS. The Greek is very clear, it says. . ."

"I know what it says! I have also read it in Greek! Although, I dare say, not as recently as you."

Rory broke into a sweat. "Yes, sir. Perhaps I'd best save my questions for a letter." "Pray God, yes, put them in a letter." He rolled his eyes. "I've no patience for your

ceaseless queries tonight." He took a deep breath. "So... you did not find my methods brutal and sadistic?"

Two actors walked past, nodded at Rory, shared knowing smiles, and continued up the stairs. Rory took a deep breath and blushed. "Please sir, may I come in?"

Jeremy gestured toward a chair, which Rory gratefully took. "I thought you were hard, sometimes, but never unjust. For instance, that chap doing *Julius Caesar*. He had no idea what he was talking about."

"Michael Tanner is not an actor. He is Eric Bates's butcher's assistant. Eric took him on as a super', then foolishly gave him one spoken line. Since he was now playing a role, he was allowed to attend my class. I am counting the days until he is gone."

"Couldn't he learn?"

"He has neither the intellect nor the discipline."

"I have both."

"I do not doubt it."

"Please sir, may I watch your class, next week?"

Jeremy blew out a deep breath and looked away. "I will not lock you out."

"But you don't want me to come. Why?"

The swish of a skirt brought Peg McCarthy into the room, carrying a costume. She saw Rory and dropped the costume on the floor. Startled and embarrassed, Rory lunged for the garment and hung it up. Peg hurried out, and Jeremy laughed until he had tears in his eyes. "So *she* is why you are still here. I thought it was out of adoration for me."

Rory wanted to sink through the floor. The wall clock read 7:25, five minutes before the half-hour call and his banishment. "Please sir. May we speak privately?"

Jeremy groaned. "By all means."

Rory closed the door and took a deep breath. "When I arrived at the rehearsal room this afternoon, there was a good deal of sniggering from the other chaps. I'd no idea why." He smiled nervously. "I kept looking to see if I'd torn my trousers." He checked Jeremy's reaction. There was none. He swallowed and continued. "Later, Peg told me they thought I was one of. . . 'Jerry's lads.'" Jeremy's expression was grim. The seconds ticked on. "When I was at school, sir," his breathing was fast and shallow. He shook his head. "I, I must have been a randy little sod."

"It seems you still are." A smile escaped from behind Jeremy's eyes.

Beads of sweat popped out on Rory's face. He smiled weakly. "My mates and I preferred girls, but they were hard to come by." He sat back and shook his head. "We tried everything. I even remember a sponge cake incident."

"I seem to remember sponge cake." Jeremy scanned his memory. "It doesn't work, does it?"

"No, it doesn't." Jeremy was silent. Rory was about to make a final humiliating apology and leave, when the elder man spoke.

"So... you have found out that I am a sadistic bastard and a sodomite, and you are still here." Jeremy sighed long and loud. "Of course you can come to my bloody class and anything else you'd like." He pursed his lips. "I was afraid you would think less of me. I credited you falsely. I apologize."

Rory's eyes were like saucers.

There was a knock on the door. A boy's voice called, "'alf 'our, Mr. O'Connell!"

"Thank you, Matt." Rory picked up his coat as Jeremy opened the door. "It appears you have had a very full day, Mr. Cookingham. Get some rest."

"Not tonight, sir. I have an exam in the morning. I'll sleep tomorrow."

"I remember those nights." Rory looked surprised and Jeremy gently pushed him out. "Stories for another day, boy."

Chapter Sixteen

Eric Bates and Jeremy O'Connell sat in the darkened stalls, listening to a parade of young men auditioning to work long hard hours for no wages. The first few were dreadful, the fifth tolerable. "Thank You. Next Please." Jeremy's voice rang out. He crossed off the first names, and put a question mark by the fifth: Courtney Adams.

A slight, fair-haired young actor in tights and an Elizabethan tunic walked gracefully onto the stage. Seeing something high on the stage-right curtain, he hurried toward it, stopped, smiled, and took a deep breath.

"*But soft! What light through yonder window breaks?*
It is the east, and Juliet is the sun."

Eric sat to attention. "What's his name?"

Jeremy glared at the paper. "Rory Cook."

"*It is my lady, O, it is my love!*"

Eric broke into a smile. "He's delightful."

"Yes, he is."

"*See, how she leans her cheek upon her hand!*"

Jeremy clenched his jaw. "The little shit."

Surprised, Eric glanced at Jeremy, then back at Rory. "Do you know him?"

"I do."

"Good."

"No. It is not good."

Rory finished and left the stage.

Eric stood up. "We'll have him."

"We will not."

"You're daft. We haven't heard a better audition in years, even from seasoned actors."

Jeremy shook his head. "Eddy!"

The stage-manager ran on-stage. "Yes, sir."

"Please send Mr. Cook to Mr. Bates's office. Keep Mr. Adams here, and send the others home."

"Yes sir."

Jeremy's heart pounded. "Trust me, Eric. Very shortly, all will become clear."

A few minutes later, Rory Cook stood to attention as Eric and Jeremy walked up the stairs. Rory smiled hopefully. Jeremy gave a cool nod and went inside. Eric said, "Mr. Cook, please come in."

Once inside, with the door closed, Jeremy hissed through clenched teeth. "How dare you! You insolent brat. After all I've said."

Rory lurched back in his chair. "We never spoke of this, sir."

"After all I've written, then. Have you no respect?"

"I've only the greatest respect, sir. I tried to do everything you teach. Wasn't I any good?"

Eric spoke up. "You were splendid." He sat behind his desk. "Sit down Jerry and tell me what the bloody hell this all about."

Rory sat up. "Well sir...,"

"Not a word." Jeremy glared at him and turned to Eric. "Mr. Cook, as he now calls himself, is a first-class student reading Law at Oxford. While he has a great academic interest in the theatre, and..." he gritted his teeth, not wanting to admit, "...considerable talent as an actor, he is not, and should not ever, become accustomed to living as a poor man. Since he would be joining us as an apprentice, receiving no wages, life here would be quite impossible."

Eric looked at the beautiful cut of Rory's suit and the neat trim of his hair. This was not a chap who could share a bed with other penniless apprentices. "Mr. Cook, your audition was very good and I want you to join our company. If you came aboard, how do you propose to live?"

Rory swallowed. "My father gives me a generous allowance, sir. More than enough to live on."

Eric nodded. "And this allowance will continue, if you left Oxford?"

"Yes sir."

Eric smiled. "Well then, Jerry. I see no problem."

Jeremy glared. "You have informed your father of your intension?"

"Not yet sir. I, I thought it premature, in case you didn't want me, there would have been no need...,"

"No need to upset you father."

"Yes sir."

91

"And now there is?" Rory shuddered as Jeremy plowed on. "The prospect is not pleasant. The idea will not be happily received."

"I have no idea, sir. Truly."

"Come now. A lad of your intellect? I am sure you know your own father well enough to anticipate his reaction to this proposal."

Rory stared at the floor. "I must try, sir. Please, just let me try."

Eric asked, "How much time will you need?"

Sweat beads popped out on Rory's brow. "I believe there is a 7:00 train. I could be home late tonight and speak with my father tomorrow, unless he's away, then I may have to wait until the day after."

Jeremy's edict was firm. "Forty-eight-hours, Mr. Cooking… Mr. Cook." He checked his watch. "It is now 4:52. You are to report back to Mr. Bates on Thursday by 5:00, but I sincerely hope that you will not. If you have not returned by that time, that other chap will be engaged in your place. Eric, is that agreeable to you?"

Eric shrugged. "I had hoped to get the new man on stage by next week, but I'll wait a couple of extra days."

"Is that agreeable, Mr. Cook?"

"Yes sir. I'll be back Thursday, before 5:00."

Nottingham

The train pulled into Nottingham station at ten minutes before midnight. Yellow gaslights shed ghostly beams over the narrow platform.

"Mister Rory? Is that you, sir?" A carriage driver searched through the fog.

"Here I am, Olins. Glad you got my wire." They walked to the waiting carriage. "Is my father at home?"

"Yes, sir. He's expecting you."

"What's his mood?"

"Well sir, to be honest," he spoke as an old friend, "grain prices are not what he would like."

"Damn!" Rory beat a fist against his thigh.

They reached the house and a young footman opened the door. "Welcome home, Mister Rory. Cook's waited up. . ."

"Thanks, but I don't need anything. He glanced at his dusty boots and chuckled silently. An elegant row of shoes and boots waited in his dressing room. After today he might be a penniless beggar, but he didn't have to look like one. "Olins, stay with me for a bit. The other servants can go to bed."

Minutes later, they carried a steamer trunk from the attic. "Going on a trip, sir?"

"Just getting some things for school." The trunk was quickly packed with most of Rory's clothes, labeled and sent to London.

He wasn't able to get his father's ear till dinner the next evening. It was the sort of meal Rory remembered. His mother was wrapped in aqua silk, emeralds and pearls. She sat at one end of the large polished table, tasting everything, but eating very little. Rory, handsome in evening clothes and miserably nervous, gulped his food without tasting it. The Squire, austerely elegant, ate heartily, while keeping up a constant monologue. He expected his wife and son to listen attentively, laugh at his jokes, agree with his opinions and offer none of their own. With military precision, a team of servants served and cleared five courses.

The meal ended and the Squire turned to his son. "Come along, boy. Let's have a smoke and you can tell me whatever trouble you're in."

His mother sat to attention. "Trouble? Rory, darling, you never said you were in trouble."

"There's no trouble, Mother."

The Squire pushed away from the table. "Whatever it is, I'll see it right."

Rory sheepishly followed his father to the smoking room. The Squire puffed contentedly on a large cigar. The smell made Rory gag.

The Squire sat back. "So, is it a woman?"

"No! No, sir." Rory was taken by surprise. "Nothing like that."

"It's certainly not your academic work. By God, the glowing reports I receive from your dean. It seems they expect you'll be running the place one day." He puffed proudly. "Wouldn't be bad for a chap in your position. Certainly make your mother proud."

Rory flinched. "I hate it, sir. I'm sorry, but I truly do."

"Good, then you'll excel just to finish faster." He smiled and flicked an ash. Rory rolled his eyes, but his father pretended not to notice. He leaned back, examining his cigar. "You were a remarkable little boy."

Rory looked up.

"You probably don't think I noticed the way you struggled to keep up with your brothers. Even as a little mite, you fought and scratched and used your wits to get whatever they had." He laughed. "You weren't about to, 'wait until you were old enough,' for anything." He slapped his thigh. "You were so damn good at everything. You've always made me proud."

Rory was amazed. He had never heard his father talk like this.

The Squire puffed on his cigar. "I'd never tell your brother," he flicked another ash, "but I wish you were my heir."

Rory gasped.

"Jamie's a good lad. He'll do fine, but, my God," he puffed contentedly, "what you could do with this estate. Ah well," he shook his head. "It wasn't to be. Since God's not given you a fair share, you'll need a rich wife." He sat back, waiting. Rory looked miserable but said nothing. The Squire poured them each a glass of port. "So, if it's not a girl, who's Peg McCarthy at His Majesty's Theatre?"

Rory gasped and put his head in his hands.

"You didn't really think my servants would allow an expensive steamer trunk to leave this house without informing me?"

"It's a long story, sir."

"I'm listening."

Rory told his story. The Squire listened calmly, without comment. He seemed to understand his son's passion and his longing. Rory finished and the Squire casually drained his glass. "Your mother's been waiting too long. Let's go and join her." He did something he had never done before. He put a hand on his son's shoulder, looked him in the eye and spoke softly. "I'll say this once. Tomorrow you're back at Oxford, or you're out of this family, forever. Your university fees are paid until the end of the semester. Go back and we'll forget the entire incident."

*

Thursday at 2:00, Rory's train pulled into Oxford Station. He'd have to pack his clothes and books, find a porter and get back in time for the 3:30 to London. He'd leave his cases at St. Pancras, grab a cab and report to Eric Bates before 5:00. The only thing his father had allowed him to take out of the house was a battered school bag. Into it, Rory had rolled a clean shirt, three collars, underclothes and ties. In his pockets were gold

94

cufflinks, jeweled studs, tie pins and a few pounds his mother had filched from her husband's dresser drawer. She had no money of her own.

It was a short walk from Oxford Station to his residence. He ran upstairs two at a time, started to put the key in the door and stopped. A note was tacked to the door.

By order of the purser:

This room is to remain locked until further notice.

Rory blinked, tried his key and pounded the door. His heart raced as he leaned against the wall, frantically deciding what to do. He couldn't go to London with only the clothes on his back. That was impossible. His father had won. Exhausted, he sighed deeply and slowly walked toward the purser's office. He'd wire his father. They would unlock the door. He could simply relax and continue his studies. It was simple. Each slow step seemed like a walk on hot coals. His heart pounded. Sweat ran down his neck. When he was almost at the office, he froze, then started running in the opposite direction. Within sight of the station, he could see the 2:30 train ready to leave for London. Holding his book bag like a rugby ball, he charged the last two hundred meters, and leap onto the moving train.

Chapter Seventeen

July 1903

Robert Dennison waited for the headmaster of Heathhead School to return from lunch. He sat on a hard bench in a long hall in the administrative building, clutching his art portfolio and breathing hard. Nervous sweat soaked his shirt, and he laughed at himself. He was twenty-six-years-old, applying for a master's position, but felt like a schoolboy waiting for a canning. At worst, the headmaster would send him packing, and he would have to seek employment elsewhere.

A gray-haired, well dressed, bearded gentleman walked up, offering his hand. "Mr. Dennison? I'm Dr. Theodore."

Robert sprang to his feet, smiled anxiously and shook the hand. "How-do-you-do, Headmaster?"

"This way, please." Dr. Theodore walked into his large study, then moved behind his desk.

Robert hastily followed. Quickly as possible, he opened his portfolio, pulled out two miniature landscape oil paintings, and placed them on the desk.

Dr. Theodore looked startled. "I'm sure those are very pleasant, but I have little knowledge of art. A colleague has assured me that the Academie Julien is a fine school, so your accreditation is more than adequate."

"Thank you, sir, but I didn't only study at the Julien. I was a private pupil of Paul Serusier. The brush strokes on this canvas show his influence. The technique is very different on this second canvas, which I painted in the style of the Acadmie...,"

"Thank you," the headmaster interrupted. "Please sit down." He sat behind his desk, ignoring the paintings.

Robert apologetically tucked his canvases back into his case.

"My secretary has informed you of the wage and responsibilities?"

"Yes, sir."

"And you find them satisfactory?"

"Yes, sir. But, I haven't seen my lodgings or the art studio."

"Of course. You will find the first masters' house immediately to the right, when you leave this building. The art master's room is on the top floor. Next to the masters' houses are academic buildings, then lodging houses for the boys. The art studio is on the other side of the river. That is the girl's side.

"When you cross the footbridge, the chapel and great hall will be on your left. Nine lodging houses will be to your right. Past the last house, just before you reach the woods, you will find the art studio. It is a small stone structure with large windows. You cannot miss it. After our interview, you may tour the grounds at your leisure.

"Most of the staff are away on holiday. They are a friendly lot, so feel free to ask questions." He looked at the frayed cuffs on Robert's suit and the rough cut of his hair. "Should you desire an advance on your salary, to better prepare your wardrobe, my secretary will arrange it."

"Thank you, sir." Robert felt himself color. He had washed and shaved that morning, but his suit was shabby, and his shoes were lined with cardboard.

The headmaster folded his hands and pursed his lips. "Mr. Dennison, I will be direct. Heathhead School educates upper-class boys who are too slow to be accepted at Harrow or Eton. While we provide an adequate education, we do not pretend to compete. Some of our boys continue into our college or other universities. Most go home to work in their families' businesses, are commissioned into the military, or the church." He shrugged with boredom. "While we try to keep enrollment at four-hundred, ten years ago, admissions dropped dangerously low. To keep the school from closing, my predecessor opened our doors to a small number of young ladies. Our girls' school now has nearly ninety students and a twofold purpose. Number one: it has kept us solvent. Number two: since most of these boys are not society's choicest, it provides them with a selection of eligible young ladies."

Robert understood the headmaster's code: girls did not need to be educated.

The headmaster droned on, "Upon graduation, many of our young ladies are betrothed to our young men... or other members of their families." He sat back shaking his head. "Last year, one of our university bound men paid court to one of our girls. They adored each other. The parents approved and the match seemed secure. Much to her despair, practically on her wedding day, the bride discovered that she had been betrothed, not to her sweetheart, but to his older brother." He sighed. "Oh well, no matter, back to you, sir."

Robert caught his breath. "How terrible... for everyone."

The headmaster shrugged it off. "We only engaged an art-master to teach our young ladies. Young men should be kept at their academic pursuits, and relax with the physical rigors of sport. Those who insist on quiet recreation are encouraged to study music. Singing can be beneficial for the lungs, and skill at the piano will always make one popular at parties. Spending days toying with paints and canvas, only to hang an ornament on the wall, seems a dreadful waste of time."

Robert's whole body tensed, but he kept still.

"There are, however, always a few boys who wish to study art. Their fathers select their classes and pay the fees, so they study what they please. We tried holding separate classes for boys and girls, but there were too few boys to schedule around their important classes."

Robert's eyes widened. "So, my classes will be a mix of boys and girls?"

"I know it is unusual, but there is absolutely nothing to concern yourself about. The art studio is one large room with windows on three sides. Everything that goes on inside is visible from the outside. The students feel rather like fish in a bowl, so there has never been any misconduct. Male and female students are all encouraged to associate at chapel, Sunday dinners, and special functions. Those are more than sufficient opportunities. You need not concern yourself about fraternization."

Like hell! Robert's pulse quickened. He liked this less and less. First, he had been insulted, told his training and skills were worthless; next, he was expected to child-mind sexually budding adolescents using the studio as a rendezvous point. Either the headmaster was a very good liar or the boys were all nancies.

He forced a good natured laugh. "Well, if I had gone to this school, I never would have left the art studio. How old are these students?"

The headmaster ignored his joke. "Twelve to seventeen. Some turn eighteen during their last year. The boys that go on to the college are, of course, older." The headmaster clenched his fist. "This year, we have a girl enrolled in college. I am dead against it, but my masters convinced me to let her try."

Robert left the headmaster's office and carried his portfolio to the top floor of the master's house. There were two attic rooms. One door had a name plate reading "Longworth." The second door was open and had no name plate. He assumed it was the tiny room for the lowly art-master. The ceiling sloped, but he could stand upright and turn around without bumping into the narrow bed, the wash stand, or the wardrobe. An adequate supply of coal waited in the bin, next to the small stove, and the one window looked onto a huge elm tree. He nodded with approval. It was all right. He could live here.

Taking his portfolio, he left the masters' house and followed the headmaster's directions. He passed ivy covered academic buildings and neat lodging houses, all cut from the same stone. They were framed by manicured gardens and lawns. The grounds were so beautiful, he guessed that the gardeners earned more than the art-master.

To his left was the shallow river, separating the boy's side from girl's side. Across the river, he could see the stone chapel and the great hall. He walked across the narrow wooden bridge, then turned right, down a gravel path, past the nine girls' lodging houses. Each house had a name over the door. The last one, Nicholas House, had a garden full of brilliant sunflowers.

A slim woman, shorter than many of the tall flowers, wearing a long green gardening smock, was bent over, weeding. She and Robert exchanged greetings, as he walked by, and continued a hundred yards to the edge of a thick wood.

Just as the headmaster had described it, there stood a small stone building with huge windows on three sides. A skylight glimmered on the slanted slate roof. It really was like a fish bowl. He guessed that the light inside would be marvelous. The gravel path faded into a dirt path, leading to the studio's front door. It was locked. He left his portfolio and walked around the building, looking in through the windows.

The lady gardener walked towards him, with a sturdy key. "You'll need this, young man." Her complexion was fair and her absolutely blue-black hair was pulled back into a fashionable chignon.

Robert broke into a smile. Henna hair colorants came from the Far East. They were very fashionable on the continent, but he had never seen

English women use them. From a distance, this petite woman had looked young. As she came closer, he saw she was old enough to be his mother. Her step was light and fluid, and her long skirt hung unfashionably straight around her slender hips. Her manner seemed not quite European, and definitely not British. He imagined her as a sparkling debutant, somewhere in Queen Victoria's Empire, but where?

Her upper-class voice had a crisp nasal twang. "I am Mrs. Carrots, Nicholas House Mistress and mathematics-mistress." He flinched and she laughed. "Yes, young sir, our young ladies actually learn their figures. You must be the new art-master." She smiled and offered her hand.

He chuckled at her joke and shook her hand. "I'm Robert Dennison, how-do-you-do?" He took the key. "I haven't accepted the post, but I expect I'll have to..." He bit his tongue, remembering he was speaking to a member of staff. "That is... it is a fine post. I am delighted it has been offered."

Unconvinced, she raised an eyebrow.

Feeling embarrassed and wondering if she would report his rude remark to the headmaster, he fumbled with the lock, and opened the door.

She marched in ahead of him. "I had better see if it needs cleaning. We had a lot of rain the last week of term. Dirty shoes can leave a mess."

Robert took his portfolio, followed her in, and stopped. "This is beautiful." The room was bright with sunlight. Blond wood walls bordered enormous windows on three sides of the single square room. "From the outside, I never guessed there was this much space." Brilliant sunlight streamed through the high skylight onto sturdy easels and drawing tables. He placed his portfolio on a table and looked for supplies.

Mrs. Carrots inspected the floors and the cold water sink. "Filthy. Just as I suspected. It will be spotless by the start of term. Not to worry."

"I am not worried, ma'am, believe me. I've spent eight years in shabby Paris lofts. This is magnificent."

Built into the fourth wall were rows of long shallow drawers. He opened each one, and was thrilled to find oil paints, water colors, brushes, pastels, clay-molding tools, plaster mix, charcoal sticks, pencils, and every variety of paper.

"I can't believe it. Most of these are brand new." A long cupboard held a roll of canvas, five feet tall and three feet wide, with pre-cut boards, ready for mounting. Near the door, rows of clothes hooks hung empty. "Are these for smocks?"

Mrs. Carrots nodded. "There are dozens. Still in the laundry, I expect." She studied Robert. "I am glad you're pleased. The last art-master filled these cupboards to impress the parents, but then he was afraid to let the girls dirty their hands."

Robert shook his head and closed the last drawer. "Well, anyone afraid of getting his or her hands dirty shouldn't study art. I'd chuck out a student who... Oh, I can't chuck anyone out, can I?"

She laughed and shook her head. "No, you can't. If tuition is paid, lessons must be given, regardless of the student's interest or ability. Imagine my task: inspiring young ladies, with nothing on their minds but dances and trousseaus, to love the intricacies of mathematics. I do it every day."

She stood proudly. "Most people think girls from affluent families are good for nothing but entertaining and making babies." He choked and she smiled mischievously. "Their heads are just as good as their brother's, often better. But they need discipline." She saw his portfolio. "May I see your pictures?"

"Oh, yes. Please." He quickly opened his case. "The headmaster didn't even want to look at them."

She pursed her lips. "That doesn't surprise me."

Robert spread two miniature oils, two pastels, and two water colors across one of the tables.

She studied them carefully, one after the other. "This is your first teaching job?"

He started to panic. "Y'Yes, but I'I'm sure I can teach well enough...,"

"To judge from these samples, you will be an exceptional art-master. The best I have ever come across."

He sighed with relief, pleased she took time to study his two oil paintings.

She nodded with approval. "Very nice contrast, here." She touched the rough canvass. "I was in love with a painter, once. He taught me a thing or two."

Robert was intrigued, "That was not in England?"

Her eyes stayed on the canvases but an impish smile spread across her lips. Her eyes sparkled. "You are correct. I was born in India and became the wife of stunningly handsome Sergeant Major Jonathan Carrots."

She took a deep breath, remembering. "My Johnny was also a gifted painter. He wanted to do nothing else. Like all second sons of wellborn fathers, he was gifted a commission in the military. A more unsuitable career was never forced upon anyone. Johnny dutifully fulfilled his post, but every free hour was filled with painting," her voice lowered, "and making love."

Robert's mouth dropped open, and she laughed. He relaxed and laughed with her. She breathed deeply and smiled with a wonderfully bright glow. "How long it has been since I have been able to speak like this." She gestured to his pictures. "I am not surprised you chose to present still-life's and landscapes. I presume your nudes are hidden away, safe from disapproving schoolmaster eyes."

He nodded. "You are correct, Mrs. Carrots." She was still smiling, so he dared to ask, "May I assume you were the Sergeant Major's favorite model?"

She sighed sadly. "I was -- clothed and unclothed. But back to you. You do not want this post. So, why are you here?" She looked at him with kind, penetrating eyes.

He looked at the floor. "How long do you have?" Expecting her to shake her head and drop the subject, he was surprised when she pulled up a chair and sat down. Relieved someone was truly interested and wanted to listen, he took a chair and sat near her.

"I am here because I need the money. My father died three months ago. He was a poultry farmer. He always did very well. I had no idea there was any trouble, but then, we hadn't communicated in years. I ran away to Paris right after school. Father wanted me to take over the business, or go to university. I wanted to paint. We had a dreadful row and I left."

"How old were you?"

"Eighteen. I was penniless, speaking schoolboy French. I knew next to nothing about painting, but told people that I was a painter and for some reason they believed me. Total strangers bought me meals, allowed me to sleep in their houses. I spent all day, every day in art galleries, museums, watching other painters, and there were a hundred: good and bad. I constantly asked questions and always listened to criticism of my own painting, even when I knew the critic was a fool. It paid off."

She nodded. "Showing respect always pays off. Besides, you have lovely manners, speak like a gentleman, and you are very easy on the eye. I am not surprised strangers were taken with you."

Robert blushed. He knew he was good-looking, but not used to compliments from elderly ladies.

Mrs. Carrots continued, "When Dr. Theodore received your application, he told me you graduated from a distinguished academy."

"Yes, thanks to Paul Serusier."

She looked startled. "He is a very famous painter."

"And a very kind man. When I was twenty, he took me under his wing. I lived in his house. I studied with him for a year, and he arranged my scholarship at the Academie Julien. When I finished, I had enough contacts to scratch out a living painting portraits. Up until three months ago, my life was wonderful. I shared a shabby loft, wore rags worse than you see me in now, ate the simplest food, but every day was full of painting, wonderful friends, and...," his insides cramped remembering, "...fantastically beautiful women."

He closed his eyes against the memories of sleek naked bodies. "Then a telegram arrived from England. Father had invested everything in a new breed of Belgium goose. A blight hit the lot. Everything was lost. He had a heart attack. Mother was left penniless. The bank took what healthy stock was left, and all the land. Now they want the house. I am her only child, so I am taking a teaching position I don't want, to pay off her debt. Tomorrow, I shall have to go to the bank and arrange a payment plan. Mother has agreed to take in lodgers."

He stopped momentarily, buried in self-pity. Glancing at the roll of canvas, then looking into the eaves and seeing dozens of empty drying shelves, he felt an adrenaline rush. "Mrs. Carrots, do you think anyone will mind if I used some of these supplies for my personal use?"

"I don't think anyone will even notice. Personally, I would love to watch you paint. Having a real artist on the premises should please the parents no end."

"And perhaps pay me for portraits of their children?"

She raised an eyebrow and thought for a moment. "Might do, after you've established yourself. Perhaps after a year."

Robert looked discouraged, then caught his breath. "There's something else." His mouth was dry with excitement. He hurried to the corners of the room, studying the storage spaces. "Last year, a London art dealer, Daniel Gildstein, came to Paris. He offered me a show. He was willing to pay for shipment of my paintings, against profits from sales, but his gallery was booked two years in advance.

"I contacted Mr. Gildstein the moment I returned to England, and just yesterday, he telegraphed that he had a cancellation for January. My paintings are still in Paris. I thought I would have no place to store them, let alone finish some, and then varnish and mount others, but I have that space here. With teaching six-days-a-week, it will be a tremendous amount of work, but..." He nervously bit his lip. "Do you think I could possibly teach and work on my own...,"

"I think you can do anything you set your mind to. How can I help?"

Tears of gratitude flooded his eyes as he gazed around the studio, imagining his paintings hanging on these pristine walls. "I'm not sure. The very idea is overwhelming. First off, I need to cable Paris and have my friend arrange for packing and shipping. Then I need to cable Mr. Gildstein for the money. When the pictures arrive, I'll need to sort and select... I'm not even sure I have enough pictures for an entire show. I may be short...,"

"If this show of yours is a success, you will be leaving us?"

His heart raced. "I'm not expecting miracles."

"Good! I want you here for a while. My girls need someone to inspire them." She walked up to him, squeezed his arm, and looked into his handsome dark eyes. He stared down into hers, bright and shining. "You are a real artist, not the silly excuse that usually passes for an art-master." She shook her finger. "Teach them, Mr. Dennison. Teach them to see, the way you see. I am not saying they will become artists, but they might see more of the world, if you teach them how."

Impressed with her dedication, he smiled. "I'll do my very best. I promise."

"Good! Now..." She stood back and looked him up and down. "Cut your hair, take an advance on your salary, and get a new suit."

He swallowed.

"How old are you?"

"Twenty-six."

"Hmm… You look younger and that is not good. Do something to make yourself look older. It won't be easy to command the respect you'll need and deserve. You can keep that studio key. I have another. If your pictures are to arrive before the beginning of term, you can ship them in my care: Amelia Carrots. I promise they shall be stored safely until you return."

She paused, considering. "I was dreading another school term -- another four months of adolescent tears and traumas. I believe your presence will cheer my life a good deal. And please, when we are in private, call me Amelia. I haven't heard my name spoken by a man in a long time. I miss hearing it."

Robert chuckled. "Thanks, A-m-elia. It's a beautiful name."

She beamed. "It is, when a man says it. Good bye, and welcome aboard." She turned on her heel and walked briskly away. Robert watched her go. She seemed to grow younger as she sprinted down the path, back to her sunflowers.

Robert spun back and studied the wonderful storage spaces. There was more than enough room for his pictures, but they had to be meticulously organized. He took drawing paper and quickly sketched every detail of the studio. His pictures would arrive in large wooden crates. Once they were opened, every drawing, painting, and pastel must be carefully stored where he could find it instantly. Most of the time, the studio would be filled with noisy students. Every private moment would be precious.

Before Robert left the school, he went back to Dr. Theodore's secretary and took an advance on his salary. The next day he found a reasonably priced tailor and ordered a new suit. Counting every penny, he decided to wait for a barber till the start of the school term. The next morning, instead of shaving his entire face, he started growing a moustache.

Chapter Eighteen

August 1903

Like a Sergeant Major inspecting the troops, Anthony Roundtree slow-marched around the servants' hall. He was now forty, short and thin. Gray streaks spread through his dark hair, down his temples, and along his sideburns. Heavy lines cut deep around his mouth creating a perpetual frown. Standing to attention, the cook, the scullery maid, two parlor maids, the houseman, the footman, coachman/groom, and groundskeeper formed a straight line. Lillian and Elisa stood close together, across the room.

Roundtree continued his march. He gazed at the ceiling. "Sir John Garingham arrives tonight, so everyone has to snap to. No more lazing about. Everything must be in order."

The servants glanced at each other. For weeks, they had worked fourteen-hour days, scrubbing and starching, painting, pruning, polishing, and making the rundown estate fit for company.

Roundtree turned to the cook. "The French chef and his staff arrive tomorrow at midday. This is *his* kitchen for the night, so stay out of his way. If he wants help, he will ask for it." He strutted proudly. "Sir John has invited titled guests. We have never had quality people in this house, so...,"

Lillian rushed to the center of the room. "Oh, but we have, Tony." She smiled serenely, clutching her wrinkled fingers together. "You were too young to remember, but this house was always filled with society. Wonderful parties... elegant visitors, laughing, dancing... Even after mama died. Papa was so handsome." She giggled, "There was a never ending stream of ladies vying for his...,"

He glared at his sister. "Silence, woman!"

She pursed her lips and cowered.

"Father's been dead for twenty years and I'm tired of hearing about him. Ever since Sir John decided to host his betrothal dinner here, you have invented the most preposterous lies." He pointed a finger. "He has *not* engaged an orchestra from Vienna, or ballet dancers from Moscow, and I am very sure King Edward will be otherwise engaged."

Lillian sniffed and Elisa held her hand for comfort.

Roundtree moved down the row of servants, cruelly berating each in turn. Suddenly, he was shouting at her. "Elisa, you are to smile and say nothing. Nothing! Is that clear?"

She nodded silently.

"If anyone asks you a direct question, smile, and answer with as few words as possible. After dinner, you will sing and play. When the guests tire of *you*, you will thank Sir John for your party, say that *you* are tired, and go to your room. If the guests wish to dance, you will play the piano until *they* tire, then excuse yourself. You are not to engage in conversation. Is that understood?"

She whispered, "Yes, Father."

Pleased with himself, he commanded, "That will be all." He turned and marched up the stairs.

The cook pulled a pretty young maid aside. "Listen, Mary. Tha've not met Sir John Garingham, and y' dan want t'. 'e's the worst sort t'is."

Mary smiled knowingly. "Not t' worry. I've kept Mr. Roundtree at arm's length."

The cook shook her head. "Garingham's not Roundtree. 'e gets w' 'e wants, no matter what. There've been two maids before y', both young and pretty, both thrown in t' street w' their bellies swelled."

Mary's eyes opened wide. "Maybe they...,"

"'Maybe' nothin'. It was rape, pure and simple, and 'e'll do t' same to thee, if tha' can't stay out of 'is way."

Mary shuddered, then nodded her thanks. Hurrying back to work, she wondered how she was going to keep her distance from the master's guest of honor.

Chapter Nineteen

"Ahh...," Lillian Roundtree leaned against a high bed post and exhaled. Mary put her knee against her mistress's back, pulled the corset strings as tight as her strong young arms could manage, and tied them tight.

Lillian gasped for breath, smiling happily. "You know, dear, this is the first new gown I have had in twenty years." Mary lifted the beaded turquoise gown, amazed by its weight. She carefully lowered it over Lillian's head, then painstakingly fastened two-dozen tiny buttons up the back.

Lillian sat at her dressing table, giggling as Mary secured a garish feathered ornament into her gray-streaked, copper hair. "When I was a little girl, I used to watch my mother dress. There were parties every night. That was forty years ago."

Mary smiled. "Goodness, Miss Roundtree, forty years is a long time. I'm only sixteen." She arranged curls over her mistress's forehead and around her eyes, covering as many wrinkles as possible.

"It seems like only yesterday," Lillian sighed. "Look Mary. Look at that portrait, see how handsome my papa was."

The maid patiently obliged. Lillian talked about the painting every day. "Both of yer parents were 'andsome, Miss. You and yer brother Charles look lak twins. Miss Elisa resembles y', wiv 'er red 'air. Mr. Roundtree's t' only one wiv dark 'air."

"Charlie and I adored each other. We were as close as twins. If he had lived, he would have taken proper care of me, and made sure that I was well married. Tony lost my dowry on a horse race. He lost everything. After Charlie died, Tony inherited the estate. Visitors stopped coming. If it weren't for Sir John, we would all be in the poorhouse."

She nervously bit her lip. "Mary dear, do you want to know a secret?" The maid bent low to hear Lillian's whisper. "I don't like Sir John Garingham. He has been generous, looking after us, all these years, agreeing to marry Elisa, even though she has no dowry, but he is not nice with women. I don't like him." Lillian's eyes glazed over.

Mary stood back. Her heart pounding.

Upstairs in the old nursery, a maid helped Elisa dress. Lillian, swathed in violent turquoise, waltzed in and stared at her niece. "Oh, my darling. You look like an angel." She turned a full length mirror toward Elisa, and the girl grimaced.

Two dozen hairpins stabbed painfully, forcing her thick copper hair to remain in place. "I don't care how it looks. It hurts." She closed her eyes, whispering, "Dear God, please let this night be over. Tomorrow I can go back to school. Just let me live through the next few hours."

She had worn a variety of corsets, but this modern, one piece undergarment was a new kind of torture devise. The thinnest strips of whalebone, exquisitely stitched into a silk frame, extended into a hooped petticoat, falling like a graceful bell, slicing into her slender waist and hips. Her bruised ribs were pinched and sore.

Over the corset, the maids threw a silk slip and finally a diaphanous Paris gown, with yards of stiff pink organdy. Elisa's small bosoms were scratched, squeezing up against a coarse ruffle. Elisa held the bodice closed, while the maid stood at the back, pushing tiny silk buttons through loops of fine thread. With each closure the organdy cut deeper into Elisa's shoulders.

"This is intolerable!" Gasping for breath, she reached to pull it free.

Lillian threw up her hands. "No, dearest. Please. You mustn't." Her hands flew over her mouth. "Sir John went to great trouble procuring that gown. You must pretend to be happy. Please, my angel!"

At the mention of Sir John Garingham, Elisa stopped struggling. She clenched her jaw. "Of course, Aunt. I shall smile and pretend to be happy. I always pretend to be happy." Her chin shook as she forced back tears.

"Don't cry!" Her aunt was frantic. "You'll ruin your face."

"Does it matter?" Roughly wiping her eyes, Elisa winced as she bent a bruised wrist.

Lillian hurried over with long pink gloves. "He won't see those bruises under these." She carefully pulled a glove over Elisa's fingers and up her arm.

"Why shouldn't he see the bruises? He made them."

A mixture of anger and fear set Elisa's heart racing. The night before, she had been called to dinner. When she started down the stairs, Sir John was on the landing. She turned to run back up, but he leapt after her, grabbed her arm, pushed her against the wall, and forced his mouth onto hers. She resisted and he snapped her wrist.

She opened her mouth to scream with pain and he pushed his tongue between her teeth, his knee between her legs, and his other hand over her breast, holding her prisoner. She fought to spit out his slimy tongue, but he was too strong. She tasted his bitter, tobacco fouled saliva, gagged, then swallowed, and finally stood still.

He released her and leaned against the banister, smiling victoriously. A servant heard the scream and ran to her aid. When he saw it was Sir John, he turned and quietly left. Elisa's heart raced as she leaned against the wall, breathing hard, blinking back tears. She felt helpless and violated. That monster was to be her husband. She wanted to die.

Garingham had snickered softly. "Taming you will be a delight, my little shrew." She stared with frightened eyes, and he chuckled some more. "You *will* learn to obey me."

Elisa forced out a whisper, "My Lord, I already obey you. And you already do everything you could possibly want."

He laughed loud and long. "Everything I could possibly want? My, my. What a charming little innocent you are." He leaned close enough so she could see his discolored teeth and smell the grease in his hair. "After we are married, I will teach you to do a great many new things – things beyond your wildest imaginings. And, all the while, you will bear me strong, healthy sons." He ran his fingers around her throat.

She closed her eyes, wondering if he was going to choke her.

"Oh, yes. Your looks and temperament will give me just the sort of boys I want." He squeezed her breast so hard it hurt. When she winced, he chuckled and left her alone.

Finally allowing her tears to flow, she sunk down onto the stairs. Only then did she feel the throbbing pain in her sprained wrist.

*

Snapped back from the horrid memory, Elisa heard her aunt chattering. "Your wrist will be fine in a few days, dear. It is your own fault, after all. Sir John said you rejected his endearment."

"Endearment? Is it endearing to be left bruised and hurting every time he touches me? He handles his horse with more gentleness." Elisa closed her eyes and clenched her jaw. "As you have always said, Aunt, 'he is my betrothed. He has the right.'" She pleaded, "Why does he want to marry me? He doesn't care for me at all."

Her aunt scolded, "It is not your business to question 'why.' A girl with no dowry must be grateful when any man agrees to marry her, especially a man of means."

The maid spoke in a frightened whisper. "He does like you, Miss. I seen the way 'e watches y'."

Elisa shuddered. "He likes the way I look. He doesn't like *me*."

Her aunt buttoned the insides of Elisa's pink gloves. "Young ladies should be seen and not heard. You question everything. It is most unseemly. It is a pity Sir John does not enjoy music. You play and sing so sweetly." She finished the buttons and stood back to view the completed picture. "Once you are mistress in your own home, he will treat you differently, with more respect."

Elisa sighed sadly. "You have just made up another pretty story, Auntie. It will be no different, or it will be worse. I shall be totally under his control, a prisoner in his house, a slave he can torture...,"

"Stop talking nonsense!" Lillian frantically fluffed Elisa's organdy skirt. "Sir John will want to show off his beautiful young wife. In a year or two, you will be blessed with a child. Then...,"

"Blessed? With *his* child?" Elisa moved close to Lillian, whispering frantically. "He said he would teach me to do things beyond my wildest imaginings. What sort of things? Please tell me, Auntie. What did he mean?"

"Ohhhh!" Suddenly faint, Lillian held out her arms, dramatically starting to fall. Since this was a regular occurrence, the maid calmly helped her to a chair and pulled a vial of smelling salts from her pocket. She plucked out the stopper and held the tiny glass under her mistress's nose. Lillian inhaled, jerked her head, then stood up, fluttering her hands. "Come, child. It is time to go down."

Taking as deep a breath as her corset allowed, Elisa started towards the door.

Before she reached the stairwell, Lillian caught her arm, held her close, and whispered, "Dearest girl, I didn't mean to scold. Please believe that whatever your married life will be like, it will be far better than the life of a spinster sister, dependent on her brother's charity."

Elisa wondered if this were true. Her chest heaved as she blinked back tears. She kissed her aunt's cheek, forced a smile, gracefully lifted her skirt, and walked down the stairs like a perfect lady.

An hour later, the dining room was bright with candle light reflecting off crystal, porcelain, and silver. Raucous laughter gushed from Sir John Garingham and his two-dozen middle-aged guests. Elisa sat in the middle of a long banquet table, toying with beautiful looking food prepared in her own kitchen by a French chef she had never met. Next to her, Sir John ate with gusto. Every few moments he leered down her cleavage. His beautiful tail coat, the elegant lace on his shirt, his jeweled studs and cufflinks, could not hide the hollows of his aging skin.

Through yards of hoops and organdy, Elisa felt his hand, under the table, probing the folds of her skirt. She clutched her knees together, swallowing a scream. At one end of the table, Lillian flirted with a stranger. Did her aunt still dream of getting married? She would gladly give up Sir John. Her father sat at the other end, laughing, gorging himself on venison and truffles. He would finally be rid of his vexing daughter. She had never seen him look so happy.

Roundtree raised his glass, stood and nearly lost his balance. "Ladies and gentlemen!" Glassy-eyed, he swayed from side to side. "You all know my dear friend, Sir John Garingham."

Cheers of, "Hear! Hear!" came from around the table.

"Well...," he forced his eyes to focus. "He has waited a long time for my daughter to grow up."

Elisa stared at her plate, ordering herself to sit still. She only had to endure another hour at the dinner table. After that, the men would stay to smoke, and the women would retire for coffee. Later, she must sing and play, after that...

Roundtree raised his glass. "She's seventeen, Sir John. Another few months and she'll be ripe for the picking."

Garingham leaned over her. "I think she's ripe for the picking right now." Grabbing Elisa's head, he pushed his open mouth against hers.

Elisa pushed him away with all her might.

Roundtree yelled, "I give you the happy couple!"

Some guests were shocked, but many stifled laughter, watching Elisa pull violently away, nearly slipping off her chair.

The meal finished and the men rose, allowing the ladies to glide into the drawing room. Before Elisa was safely out the door, Roundtree gripped her arm, whispering, "I'll thrash you for that." He pushed her out, then returned to the other men.

Elisa braced herself against the wall. She wanted to die.

Chapter Twenty

The next time Robert Dennison boarded the train for Heathhead School, reality hit him like a slap in the face. He would not get back to Paris for years. He was going to be an English school-master, earning a tiny wage, locked inside institutional walls with children, stodgy professors, and frustrated school-mistresses. Alone in a train carriage, he leaned back into an upholstered seat, listened to the click-clacking of the iron wheels, and nervously reviewed his plans.

- I'll be sending most of my wages to pay off mother's debts, but I get room-and-board at the school. If my expenses don't exceed shaving soap and tooth powder, I shall be all right.

- All my pictures should have arrived from Paris. God bless my friends for sending them, and that remarkable Amelia Carrots, for seeing to them at the school. I hope they are undamaged. When they're ready for display, I'll ship them to London C.O.D.

- Mother should be fine. She says she doesn't want lodgers in her house, but it would be worse if she were alone with nothing to do. The workers are nice chaps. They don't expect a lot of service. They'll pay a fair rent, and wire me if there's any trouble.

- This short haircut looks better than I thought it would. The moustache is almost thick enough to be convincing. At least I'll look older than the students.

He studied the seams of his new suit. It was simply made, but a serviceable dark-gray that would hide dirt. He planned to wear his old trousers in the studio, and take off his new shirt cuffs the minute he stepped through the door. If the parents did not like their art-master in shirtsleeves and a smock, too bad. In Paris, he wore rags... or nothing at all.

He smiled, remembering his former life. The steadiest part of his income had come from modeling nude, sometimes for schools, often in private sessions for rich women artists. Since sex was readily available to everyone, he only indulged his patrons when it pleased him. He had not had a woman since he arrived back home, nearly four months ago.

English girls were a very different breed. So were their parents. When he was a boy, his pastor had preached that masturbation caused blindness. Robert laughed to himself. If this were true, his painting career would be over before it began.

The train slowed and he groaned. *Again*? They seemed to stop at every crossroad.

"Settle Station!" The conductor blew his whistle and waved his flag. " 'ere y' go, Miss." The compartment door opened, and the conductor helped a tall young girl step in. When the door was closed, she lowered the window and spoke to an older woman standing on the platform. The girl and the woman had slender builds and copper hair, so Robert assumed they were mother and daughter.

The woman fluttered her hands. "You're sure you'll be all right, dearest? Traveling alone? I wanted to come with you, but your father will wake with a dreadful headache, and after last night's party…,"

"I'll be fine, Auntie. It's only a couple of hours, and the train will be full of other students. You know they always take us straight to the school. Do stay in the village, today. Father will be so cross. Perhaps, if he sleeps it off…,"

Steam from the engine billowed past, as huge iron wheels groaned slowly, moving the massive locomotive and passenger cars behind it. The girl clutched the window to keep from falling. The woman trotted next to the train. "Take care, Elisa darling."

"You take care, Auntie. I'll write soon. Please…" Her last words were lost in the scream of the steam whistle. As the train picked up speed, the girl awkwardly closed the window and sunk into the nearest seat. Robert watched from behind his newspaper. The girl looked weary and unhappy, as she leaned back and closed her eyes. A few minutes later, she jumped up, lowered the window, and gasped for air.

Robert dropped his paper. "Are you all right?"

"Yes, thanks. I'm fine." The last word caught in her throat as she stayed gazing at the lovely countryside. Forcing a nervous smile, she closed the window, braced herself against the rocking motion, and unbuttoned her coat. As it slid off her shoulders, Robert stood, took the coat and folded it onto an overhead rack. She stared at the floor, stammering, "Y' You are very kind to help me, sir. Thank you." Keeping her eyes lowered, she sat back down and unpinned her hat.

115

"My pleasure." Sitting back, pretending to read his newspaper, he studied Elisa's brilliant copper hair, framing huge green eyes, unnaturally pale lips, and flawless white skin. Dark circles ringed her eyes. She looked ill. She also looked like a renaissance angel. He had never seen more symmetrical features. He guessed she was about sixteen, but taller than most girls. His eyes slipped lower. She was practically built like a boy. Her lovely frock hung loose, and she was not wearing a corset. She was not coughing, so perhaps her illness was not serious.

She carefully pulled off her gloves, wincing with pain as she bent a bruised wrist. Robert recognized the bruises as finger marks, and clenched his jaw. He wanted to thrash every man who battered a woman. If this was Paris, he could take her to his loft, get some food into her, peel off that lovely frock, make slow, passionate love to her, then nurse her back to health.

Groaning with desire, he sat back and crossed his legs. What the hell was he doing back in this country? If he even touched her, he would be drawn and quartered, and she sent home to the stinking sod who had battered her.

At the next station stop, the compartment door flew open. A stocky, dark-haired girl with eyeglasses stood triumphantly on the threshold. "Elisa!"

"Lucy Ann!" The girls hugged, giggled and both talked at once. Robert watched from behind his paper. He was pleased to see Elisa smile. Slight color flushed her cheeks, making her even more beautiful. The girls were a curious pair. The plain one looked like a school-mistress in training.

Elisa's eyes were bright. "Oh, Lucy, you're letter was astonishing. I can't believe you're going to be a doctor."

"For now, I'm just going to be in college. I have to handle the lessons and pass the exams. We'll see about the rest, later. Dr. Theodore's dead against me. He'll make everything doubly difficult." She took off her spectacles and rubbed a red mark on the bridge of her nose.

Elisa scowled. "But that is not a bit fair. You already do better than the boys. He should be proud that a woman wants to make her own way, and not be dependent on a man. I'd give anything to be as clever as you are."

Lucy chuckled. "You're already too clever, and too serious. Men don't like pretty women with brains."

Robert raised an eyebrow. *I do!*

Elisa bit her lip. "And you'll be taking classes on the boy's side. Aren't you terrified?"

Lucy Ann leaned back, carelessly squashing her dark hair, tied in a serviceable bun. "I'm nervous about the work, not the boys. I have five brothers, remember."

"I wish I had a brother." Elisa's forehead wrinkled. "I never know what to say to boys. I always make a fool of myself." Remembering the strange man a few feet away, she lowered her voice to the softest possible whisper.

Robert smiled to himself. If this was the college bound girl the headmaster was so dead against, she would give the boys a run for their money. Her lovely friend was no flutter-brain. Most pretty women surrounded themselves with fawning, plain women friends. In this case, the pretty girl admired the plain one. He liked her all the more for that.

Chapter Twenty-one

The girls arrived at Nicholas House in time to dress for dinner. Elisa raced into the waiting arms of her house-mistress, Mrs. Carrots. Since the elder lady was short and Elisa quite tall, the girl had to bend down. Mrs. Carrots felt Elisa's arms and looked at her waist. "You're very thin, dear. Just the same as last time. This holiday, you promised me you'd eat."

"Please don't be cross." Elisa smiled, grateful for the old woman's concern. "I'll eat everything, now that I'm back. It was just so horrid at home." She held out her bruised wrist.

Mrs. Carrots shuddered. She examined the injury, checked to see no one was listening, then whispered seriously. "Have the banns been posted?"

Elisa's throat tightened. "I suppose. If they haven't, they will be, after last night's engagement party, but that still doesn't mean...,"

"Of course it does, child."

Elisa whispered hopefully, "The wedding is not until June. There are a hundred young men at this school, old enough for marriage. If just one of them falls in love with me...,"

"Stop it, child! We have discussed this before. You are seventeen. You cannot disobey your father. If you were twenty-one, the law would be on your side. Until then, you must do as he wishes, and he wishes you to marry, next summer. You told me you have no dowry. The man must be extremely wealthy, to take a wife with no dowry."

"Don't men ever marry for love?"

Mrs. Carrots smiled sadly. "A few do, but it's very rare."

Lucy Ann hurried up the stairs. "Come on Elisa! We'll be late for dinner and I'm famished."

Mrs. Carrots gently pushed Elisa. "Go on, dear. Get dressed. I'll give you the name of your escort when you come down."

Elisa's face lit up. "Who do I have?"

"When - you - come - down. You're the last to arrive, so hurry. Your trunk is in your room."

"Please."

"Oh, very well." Mrs. Carrots took a card with Elisa's name on it. Turning the card over, she read, "Colin Edwards, reading medicine."

Elisa smiled excitedly. "He's going to be a doctor. Doctors can make a lot of money." She raced up the stairs.

Mrs. Carrots sadly shook her head. Minutes later, ten excited young ladies fell into line: Elisa and Lucy Ann were the last. Mrs. Carrots gave them a cursory inspection, then marched ahead. The girls followed, two by two, like goslings behind a goose, joining eight similar parties on their way to Heathhead School's opening ceremony.

When they reached the great hall, Elisa looked through the large windows, into the foyer. She grabbed Lucy Ann's arm. "Look at all those young men. We must know some from last year. Surely one of them..." She stopped herself from saying more. Lucy Ann had modern views of academia, but traditional moral values. Elisa had never told her she was betrothed to a monster and hoped to elope with anyone else who would have her.

One-by-one, the girls walked up to the door. A stuffy master bored from years of the same routine, asked each girl's name. After checking his list and matching her with her assigned escort, he called the young man's name, and sent the couple into dinner.

When Elisa was introduced to handsome Colin Edwards, her mouth dropped open. She looked up into clear blue eyes and a dazzling smile, complete with dimples. His shining golden hair looked like an angel's halo.

Colin appeared equally delighted with beautiful, slim Elisa. When he offered his arm, she curtsied, blushed becomingly, lowered her eyes, took his arm, and said nothing. Colin smirked approvingly, and Elisa was thrilled. They joined the procession of young couples entering the hall, filling up long tables. Colin held Elisa's chair, then sat next to her. As other couples joined them, Colin chatted with the boys, ignored comments from the girls, but occasionally smiled at Elisa.

She longed to join the conversation, but forced her gaze to stay low and her mouth to stay shut. If she kept still, she might keep his approval.

*

Robert Dennison arrived at the school with one thing on his mind: *Are my pictures all right?* He carried his coat and battered suitcase into the masters' house, hurried up the creaky stairs, and practically ran into a

119

slight, elderly man in a valet's uniform, sweeping the second floor landing.

"So sorry, sir." The man pulled his broom and dust pan aside. "I'm Longworth, the house steward. You must be Mr. Dennison, the new art-master."

"That's right. How-do-you-do?" Robert smiled and extended his hand.

Unused to such familiarity, Longworth stared at the hand before taking it. "I'm very well sir. Thank you, sir. It's a pleasure. Welcome to Heathhead School." As he pumped Robert's hand, a smile spread across his face. Years seemed to fall away. "I've tidied your room, sir. The water pitcher's filled, and there's a carafe and glass on your bed table. You'll 'ave clean towels and bed linens every week and fresh water every day. If y' wish a hot bath, there's a tub in the kitchen. I got to know at least a day ahead, in case the other masters want one a' the same time. There's ten o' y' in the house. The chapel bell just rang, sir, so you've only got an 'alf hour 'til dinner. Headmaster's a stickler for punctuality."

"Just as he should be. Thanks, Longworth. You're very kind."

Longworth stared apologetically at the floor. "You're the only master on the fourth floor, sir. I'm in the other room. 'ope y' don't mind bein' on the same...,"

"I'm sure you'll be excellent company. Thanks again, Longworth."

"Yer very welcome, sir. Let me know if there's anything you need."

"Will do."

At the top landing, Robert saw his name, "Dennison," in a door plate. Pleased that he was official, he turned the key in the door and pushed it open. Dropping his suitcase in front of the wardrobe, he tossed his coat on the bed, filled the water glass and drank thirstily. Pleased to see a new bar of soap on the wash stand, he emptied the water pitcher into the basin, removed his shirt cuffs, loosened his tie, and carefully washed his hands and face.

He looked into a small wall mirror, combed his hair, and spread his still new moustache hairs as far over his upper lip as they could stretch. He pulled his cuffs back on, straightened his tie, and studied his reflection. Like it or not, he was a school-master. He practiced scowling into the mirror, and burst out laughing. If frowning was a prerequisite of the job, he was lost before he even started. He left the room, deciding not to lock the door. There was nothing in there worth stealing.

Remembering Longworth's warning about tardiness, Robert hurried down four flights of stairs. Once outside, he trotted along the river path, past academic buildings and the boys' lodging houses. He crossed the bridge to the girl's side, past the girl's lodging houses, and the sunflower garden, to the art studio at the edge of the woods. Before turning from the main path, to the studio entrance, he glanced back to see young ladies come out of Nicholas House. Among them was the beautiful copper-haired girl and her academic friend. He fumbled in his pocket for the door key Mrs. Carrots had given him, then walked around the corner and hastily opened the studio door.

Four large wooden crates stood in the middle of the floor. Shipping instructions were written in French and English, and addressed to Mrs. Amelia Carrots. *Thank God, and thank you, Mrs. Carrots!* Dying to rip the crates apart and unpack his pictures, he checked for external damage. There was none. After dinner, he would change from this new suit and unpack. The chapel bell rang. He sped outside. Remembering the very valuable things in the studio, he locked the door and pocketed the key. He hurried back up the path, slipped into the great hall, and found the masters' table, seconds before the headmaster said grace.

The food arrived and Robert wolfed down bland mutton, boiled potatoes, and soggy vegetables. School food had not improved since he was a boy. At least it was free and plentiful. Straining to see around the room, he noticed a few tables with young men and young ladies together. Younger boys and girls ate at separate tables, with teachers of their same sex. The few women he could see were plain and simply dressed.

A thickly bearded master leaned across the table and spoke with his mouth full. "You're new, must be the Latin master. I'm Canterville, Maths."

Robert half-rose, extending his hand. "No. Art. I'm Rob...,"

"Art? Does one actually teach art?" Declining the handshake, Canterville waved his fork, then stabbed it back into his mutton. "Keeps the young ladies busy, I suppose."

Nine other masters mumbled their names and specialties. Most seemed put out that they were sitting with a non-academic master. Only the man next to him smiled and offered his hand. "Jenkins, Sciences. How ja do."

Smiling gratefully, Robert shook his hand. "Dennison, Art... I'm afraid."

Dr. Jenkins spoke loudly enough for everyone to hear. "Dr. Theodore told me you're a fine painter. Studied in Paris. Being a scientist, I'm interested in color spectrums. Like to learn more. Perhaps you'll be kind enough to give me a lesson."

The other masters looked confused, and exchanged troubled glances. Robert was pleased, and amused. They obviously respected Dr. Jenkins's opinions. He nodded. "You're very kind, Dr. Jenkins, and... of course. I would be delighted."

Another master spoke to no one in particular. "Hear about our lad, Malcolm Robertson? Got drummed out of the cavalry. Story is, he fell off his horse. More likely, something to do with the brigadier's wife." He coughed out a laugh, and the conversation moved to unpleasant gossip about students and faculty Robert had never met. His thoughts drifted back to his pictures. *I can hang some in the studio. There are plenty of easels. I can work in the morning, before the students arrive...*

"Do you play cricket?" A monocled classics-master glared at Robert.

Robert woke from his day dreaming. "Sorry?"

"You look fit. Do you play cricket?"

"I did. In school. It's been a long time. I don't...,"

"Capital!" He turned to a colleague. "Canterville! The art-master's mine. What's your name, again?"

"Um, Dennison."

The classics-master waved his fork. "Dennison's mine!"

"Hold on a minute, Hargrave." Canterville spat a carrot slice onto his gray beard. "I get first pick of the new men."

Robert cringed.

Dr. Jenkins whispered, "So it goes, Dennison. A minute ago they didn't want to know you. Now you're a bone between hungry dogs."

Robert stifled a laugh.

While the other men argued, Dr. Jenkins continued, "Don't worry about the cricket. Last year the faculty teams didn't organize until spring."

The headmaster stood for his annual welcoming address. There was a rattling of glasses and silverware, then silence, as everyone sat back to listen. He introduced four new masters, Robert being the last. He stood, smiled, sat down, and wished he could leave.

*

When Elisa saw Robert, the man from the train, she wanted to sink through the floor. She had totally embarrassed herself, first by nearly fainting, later by prattling with Lucy Ann. If she had known he was a school-master, she would have stayed silent, like a proper lady.

Colin grinned at Robert, whispering, "I must meet him. My father's making me read medicine, but I love to paint."

Elisa spoke for the first time. She whispered, "I love to paint." It was a total lie. She had not painted anything since she was a baby in the nursery.

Colin looked pleased. "Do you, really? How charming." He turned away, to speak to a boy at the far end of the table.

Her heart pounded. A woman should share her husband's interests, and Colin loved art. Sir John wanted her to be a lady. He made sure she had learned everything else. She could already sing, play the piano, recite, speak French, and embroider, but she had never studied art. Ladies should know how to draw and paint. The art studio was on girls' side. After dinner, Colin led Elisa from the hall, into the cool night air. There was still time before the bell rang for house-hours, so they walked by the river. Fireflies flashed in the mist, crickets chirped, and water lapped softly along the shallow river bank. Colin skimmed a stone, then stood still, his brows pulled together in thought. Elisa watched silently, wondering if he would speak.

After taking a deep breath, he finally said, "Miss Roundtree, I hope you don't think me a lout with no manners, but I was wondering…,"

Elisa swallowed. "What is it, Mr. Edwards?" She held her breath.

"You are a very sweet girl."

She exhaled.

He nervously toyed with a stone. "You're also the prettiest girl I've ever seen."

This was wonderful. She smiled demurely.

"I know we just met a couple of hours ago, but…" He took a deep breath. "Could we possibly call each other by our Christian names?"

"Oh, yes!" She sighed with relief. "Yes, please… Colin."

"There's a problem."

"What?"

"I don't know how to say your name."

"Oh, that." She shook her head. "It's a German name. It's supposed to be pronounced: El-ee-zza. Some people say El-ee-ssa. I really don't mind."

"Well, thanks, El-ee-zza." He held out his hand.

She tentatively reached for it. The chapel bell rang and she jumped back. "You'll have to run. Go quickly or the bridge monitor will give you a black mark."

"Can't I walk you back to your…?"

"No! You must hurry. Please!"

"All right." He took a few steps, then hurried back, gave her a quick peck on the cheek, and joined other young men and boys racing for the bridge.

Startled and thrilled, her fingers touched the spot he had kissed. Her mind raced. This was exactly what she had hoped for, a fantastically handsome, rich young man who might fall in love with her. She had to convince her father to enroll her in art classes.

*

As soon as Robert Dennison was able to leave the great hall, he crossed back over the foot bridge, hurried to his room, changed into his old suit, and returned to the art studio. Moonlight shone through the skylight and large windows, dimly illuminating the four large wooden crates. Heart pounding, he struck a match, held it over a wall sconce and turned up the gas. Waiting for the popping sound, he pulled his hand away, just as gas ignited with a sudden hiss. After adjusting the flame and throwing away the match, he lit a gaslight on the far side of the room, and rummaged through a drawer of framing supplies for a hammer.

Very gently, he pried opened the first crate. Biting his lip in anticipation, he removed the top boards and packing rags. Inside, like buried treasure, he found a pile of mounted canvases wrapped in individual cloths. Slowly and carefully, he slid his fingers around the first picture and lifted it from the crate. It weighed almost nothing. He eagerly held the picture under a gaslight, and scrutinized every inch. *Thank God*! It was perfect.

He allowed himself an extra moment, enjoying the image of a voluptuous nude woman smiling seductively from rumpled bed sheets. He whispered to the picture, "Who are you with tonight, Margot?"

He suddenly remembered that any passerby could see in the windows. He turned the painting toward the wall. He opened one of the floor-to-ceiling storage cupboards, climbed on a foot stool, then placed the painting on the highest shelf. After unpacking the rest of his pictures, he stored all his nudes on high shelves, where no one could see them. Street scenes, landscapes, and pictures of books, flowers, and fruits were hung on picture hooks screwed into the walls. Unfinished pictures were stored on shelves or propped on corner easels, so he could work on them when classes were not in session.

He was startled by a knock on the door. It opened and Mrs. Carrots stood on the threshold. He hurried to greet her. "Mrs. Carrots, thank you a thousand times."

She took both his hands, glanced eagerly around the room, and saw his pictures on the walls. "They arrived safely? The crates looked sound."

"They're perfect." When they had last met, she wore an oversized gardening smock. Tonight, prim and corseted in a stylish gray frock, her blue-black hair upswept in a pristine twist, she looked the part of an attractive mathematics-mistress.

She hurried to study a large painting on the wall. "This is Paris. I've never been." He eagerly watched her reaction. She stood back smiling. "It's wonderful. I can practically smell the street. There's wonderfully strong coffee, fresh rolls, putrid garbage, and a very old horse."

He laughed, "Yes, all of that, and those windows -- that garret was my home. I miss it."

She walked from picture to picture, taking time examining each one. "These are wonderful, even in this bad light. Be careful of that one, it's too low. Some child is liable to knock it off the wall."

He quickly removed it. "Right, thanks. I'll hang it higher, tomorrow." He put it on a shelf.

She pointed to the highest shelves. "Are those your nudes?"

"Yes, they're hiding." He laughed and carefully brought them down, one at a time. She moved away from the windows. He glanced out, into the dark night. "Does anyone prowl around at this hour?"

125

She studied the image and smiled. "It's doubtful, but possible. A girl in my house is fond of late night strolls through the woods. She climbs down the trellis outside her window."

"Is that allowed?"

"Not at all, but she comes from such a restrictive household, I turn a blind eye."

"Does she know that you know?"

"Certainly not. That would spoil her fun. We've no wild beasts in our wood, so I believe she is safe." She chuckled, studying the painting. "This woman is marvelous. What's her name?"

Robert sighed. "Margot."

"She's clever, I can tell, and very droll. Your special friend?" He colored red and she laughed. "There's my answer. You must miss her."

He sighed again. "I do, terribly." He exchanged her painting for another. "Here's Sonja -- A stupid girl, but very sweet."

"And very beautiful. Have you any portraits of clothed models?"

He hung his head. "No. All my clothed portraits were either commissioned, or given as gifts. It never occurred to me that I'd need any."

Mrs. Carrots raised an eyebrow. "Well, art-master, if you wish commissions, painting your students, these samples will not do."

"Spot on." He laughed, and carried the paintings back up the stepladder to their high shelves.

She yawned happily. "It's past my bedtime, but well worth it. I'm delighted you're here. Nicholas House is so close by, the girls will invite you for tea."

"That's very kind, but will they actually want me?"

"A handsome young man in a totally female abode -- what could be richer? Good night, Mr. Dennison. Don't stay too much later yourself. These walls will seem very close at 9:00, when the first children pour in."

"I believe you. Good night, Mrs. Carrots."

She waved and left.

It was after midnight when he finished storing all the empty crates high in the exposed roof beams. In a few hours, he would have to pretend to be an art-master. Fifteen wooden easels stood against a wall. He quickly grouped them in a circle, facing the center of the room, and placed high stools behind each. A single stool remained in the center of the room. Studying that stool, he turned it upside down. Four shadows spread on the floor, leaning away from four legs. *Shading and perspective. I'll see what they can do with that.*

Chapter Twenty-two

Two weeks into the term, Elisa woke up famished. She leapt from the bed, washed, dressed, and flew down stairs. Lucy Ann was already pulling on her coat. Now that she was taking classes with young men, Lucy Ann's hair was pulled back extra tight. She wore a tailored jacket and made a joke of straightening her tie. Elisa laughed, then gritted her teeth in a smile for the new girl, Meredith Locksley. Sixteen, petite, stylishly plump, with silky dark hair and huge eyes, Meredith was enrolled in dramatics. For the past three years, Elisa had been the school's unchallenged drama queen. Embarrassed by her skinny body, and tensing for competition, Elisa devoured a huge breakfast.

The day began wonderfully. She received the top mark for reciting a Shakespeare sonnet. Later, she was praised for singing, *O! For The Wings of a Dove*. That afternoon, after lessons in mathematics and French, she shuffled home, thinking she was wasting her time. She wanted to please Mrs. Carrots, but she would never be clever at math's. Her French was excellent, but Sir John hated to travel, so she would never be allowed to use it. If some other man fell in love with her, he could take her round the world. She sighed sadly. Mrs. Carrots was right. Prince Charming would never charge up on a white horse and carry her away.

She angrily kicked stones along the dirt path, not caring that she would have to clean her shoes. It was only two o'clock, so there was the added torture of a study hour at her desk, until teatime. She arrived at Nicholas House and found Mrs. Carrots sitting primly at the large parlor table, correcting mathematics homework. Elisa managed a polite if slightly hostile smile. She dragged herself upstairs to her second story room, sat at her study desk, and stared at her school books. A delicious breeze blew in her open window, and she starred out at the lush, inviting woods just a few yards away, beyond the art studio.

Lucy Ann was still in college. Her class days never seemed to end and Mrs. Carrots scolded her for studying too much. Lucy was content with her plain frocks, her plain hair, and her horrid spectacles. She spent entire days doing math's and cutting up frogs -- with boys.

Elisa sighed out loud, "Boys like her. I wish they liked me." She pictured Colin's handsome face, golden hair, and shining blue eyes. He said that she was sweet, and the prettiest girl he had ever seen.

Unable to sit still, she grabbed her poetry book, tucked it into her waist band, rolled up her long skirt, and pushed the window curtain aside. The air was deliciously cool as she climbed down the trellis. When she reached the ground, she pulled off her shoes and stockings, and ran barefoot through the moist grass. She hurried past the art studio and followed the curve of the river, until it merged into a tiny stream. Spotting her special bush, she pushed it aside and crawled into a small grotto.

The thick ground cover was cool and soft. Sunlight dappled brightly through the canopy of leaves. She lay on her back and stretched out across a carpet of heavy moss. Nature's sweet perfume was intoxicating and she joyfully filled her lungs.

She opened her poetry book and pictured Colin.

Shall I compare thee to a summer's day?

Thou art more lovely and more temperate.

She returned late for tea. Her housemates were already chomping on buttered scones. Mrs. Carrots poured, and gestured to a slip of paper on the table. "Elisa, take that to Mr. Dennison, tomorrow. Your father wishes you to study art."

Elisa's giggled. She would finally be with Colin. Her heart raced with excitement.

*

The next afternoon, the 2:00 chapel bell rang, ending Robert's class for twelve-to-fourteen-year-olds. Eleven girls hung their nearly clean smocks on hooks. The one boy's smock was filthy, so Robert tossed it into a laundry basket. Unfinished pictures were piled on one table, finished pictures on another, and hopeless attempts were crumpled into a trash bin. Taking shawls and coats off hooks by the door, they hurried out and down the path.

Robert was exhausted. He seized his fifteen minute break and collapsed into a chair. A plump, saucy twelve-year-old lingered by the door, batting her eyelashes. Robert stifled a laugh. "Good bye, Miss

Huntington. I shall see you tomorrow." The girl sighed and ran to catch up with her friends.

Robert gratefully closed his eyes. His last class was for the eldest students, sixteen and older. He heard crunching footsteps along the gravel path and groaned. That would be Colin Edwards. He was always the first to arrive. It was a shame the young man had no talent. He really loved to paint.

Colin walked through the open door, saw Robert slumped in a chair, and stopped. "Oh! Sorry, sir. I'm too early. I'll just…"

"It's all right Edwards." Robert smiled and stretched. "Time I got ready for you next lot. I'm a bit worn out, this time of day. That's all."

Colin hero-worshiped Robert enough to copy his appearance. Even though he only worked with charcoal, he dressed as if he were painting with the brightest, indelible oil paints. He hung his jacket on a hook. Then he pulled off his shirt cuffs and rolled up his sleeves. He slipped on a smock, and buttoned it down the front. "You told me you were painting at first light, sir. It must make for a very long day."

"It doesn't really. I just keep different hours than the rest of the school." Robert walked sleepily to a pile of ferns in a corner. He took three, arranged them in a tall vase, and carried it through the circle of easels to the center of the room. "I'm probably asleep when you're still deep into your studies."

"I *am* studying extra late, and for the most appalling reason. There's a girl in my classes. Can you believe it, sir? They're allowing a girl to read medicine, *and* giving her top marks. She constantly challenges the masters, asks interminable questions. They actually seem to like it. She's a veritable teacher's pet."

Robert hid his amusement. "This girl must be very clever to give you chaps a chase."

"She's not clever at all." Colin's jaw tightened. "She's cunning, like an animal. Dresses almost like a man, and she's not a bit feminine." He walked to his usual easel. "She's been lucky, that's all. I'm sure she'll wash out. It's an absolute scandal. I hope she's tossed out on her ear."

Robert whispered silently, "You should be tossed on your ear. Little snot!" He turned back and caught his breath.

Elisa stood in the doorway, smiling at Colin. She was even more beautiful than Robert remembered. She had gained weight, and her color was radiant. She politely lowered her eyes, curtsied, and handed Robert her art class enrollment slip.

Colin beamed. Since their first meeting at the opening supper, they had waved to each other across the river, sat near each other at chapel, but only exchanged a few words.

Robert read the enrollment slip. "Very well, Miss Roundtree. We're using charcoal today."

The room quickly filled with eight girls and two boys, tossing smocks over their clothes, then hurrying to claim stools and easels.

Colin hurried to Elisa. "Come over to my side. The light's best."

Thinking that Colin should play Romeo on his own time, Robert steered her to an easel on the other side of the room. "I don't think so. This is Miss Roundtree's first class. She will do better on this side."

Sure she had already committed some offence, Elisa shuddered when Robert held a smock open. Obeying at once, she turned her back and slid her arms through the sleeves. He pulled it up, and gently pushed her toward a high stool. Nervous as a cat, she joined the circle of students, all staring at the ferns.

Colin sent her a bright smile, then concentrated on his drawing. All the other students sketched busily with their charcoal sticks.

Elisa smiled back, then stared at the large piece of gray paper tacked onto the easel in front of her. She tentatively lifted a stick of charcoal, toyed with it, and watched it blacken her fingers. Grimacing, she dropped the charcoal, wiped the smudges on her smock, and stared longingly at Colin.

Robert watched her and shook his head. All she could think of was that tedious boy, and she was not happy about dirtying her hands. Making slow rounds, Robert corrected each student's work, one at a time. When he reached Elisa, her paper was bare. He raised an eyebrow and she blushed.

"I, I'm sorry, sir. I don't know what to do."

He sighed wearily. "Just draw what you see."

"But, what if I'm not any good?"

He rolled his eyes. "How long have you studied art?"

She whispered, "I've never studied."

He whispered back, "Then, how can you expect to be 'good' at something you've never done?"

She shrugged nervously.

He continued whispering. "You might be naturally good. After you've studied for a while, you'll be better. For today, just look -- think about what you see -- and mark the paper. Art isn't like math's, with right or wrong answers. It's just the artist's expression of what he... or she sees." He moved on, but kept watching her.

She took a lot of time looking around the room and out the windows. He was relieved when she finally picked up a charcoal stick and started marking the paper. At first she drew slowly, judging each stroke. Soon, she was totally involved, glancing in all directions, marking the paper with bold strokes.

It was a half-hour before Robert came around to her again. He looked at her picture and caught his breath. The paper was a chaos of lines and smudges. Some marks ran off the page, onto the wooden easel.

Startled by his return, Elisa jerked back. Seeing her blackened fingers, she gasped, dropped the charcoal, wiped her hands on her smock, then stopped when the fabric blackened.

Robert gestured to a long sink with two cold water taps. "You can wash your hands anytime you like."

"Thank you, sir." She gratefully slid off her stool and went to wash. The icy water stung, but she liberally rubbed a large cake of brown soap into her fingers. Quickly, the black was gone.

Robert studied her picture. It was remarkable. There was no technique, but she had discovered a rough form of cubism. It was reminiscent of Delaunay. He was sure she had no idea what she had done. When she returned, he was still concentrating on the drawing.

"Tell me about your picture."

She almost sobbed, "I know it isn't any good."

"I think it may be very good." A boy at the next easel strained to look, so he moved to block his view. He pointed to a tiny squiggle at the bottom of the paper, whispering, "Are those the ferns?"

She whispered back, "Yes. These are the other easels and the students drawing."

"That arrow shape? Is it the tower of the administration building?"

"Yes, and that's the headmaster. He was easy to recognize, but I wasn't sure who he was talking to."

"Then, this must be the river, and the woods, and my paintings on the walls." He gazed in admiration. "Miss Roundtree, this is extraordinary. What made you draw so much?"

"You told me to look and draw what I see."

"And you see a great deal."

"But, you had no idea what it is. That's terrible!" Her voice was a quiet wail.

"That doesn't matter. I can teach you technique, but no one can teach a person to observe the way you do. It's a gift. I'd like the other students to see this picture."

"No! Please don't. I'm so embarrassed." Tears filled her eyes.

"All right. But I'm keeping this one. Sign it." He took an eraser and carefully cleaned the lower right corner.

"But, I have a long name."

"Then initial it." When she scratched E. R., he chuckled. "Either you drew this, or Edward Rex." She couldn't tell if he was being clever or cruel, pretending her mess of a picture was good. He removed the paper and tacked up a clean one. "Class is only another few minutes. See how you can do drawing the ferns. Nothing but the ferns."

Determined to do better, Elisa picked up a charcoal stick, and took time studying the ferns.

Minutes later, the chapel bell rang. Since this was the last class of the day, some students raced out the door, but others kept drawing, or chatted with their friends. Colin walked around to Elisa, wiping his hands on his smock. He looked at her picture and laughed loudly. The page was clean, except for a few pristinely neat, curving lines, gracefully copying the curves of the ferns. "You sweet little silly thing. An entire hour has passed, and this is all you've got." He took her hand, and saw that it was nearly clean. "You haven't even dirtied your pretty fingers. How delightful!"

Elisa was thrilled. This was perfect. She was sure Colin could fall in love with her.

"Edwards?" Robert's voice boomed, "That was Miss Roundtree's second picture. You should see the first, it is extraordinary."

No! Elisa wanted to sink through the floor. She clutched her hands together and stared at the floor. Robert saw her reaction and realized his mistake. "Of course, Edwards, she should see your picture, first."

Elisa sighed with relief as Colin led her around to his easel. His drawing was nothing but ferns. He hadn't drawn the vase underneath, so they seemed to float in the air. He boasted about his use of tones and textures. Elisa pretended his words were thrilling and eagerly agreed with everything. When he invited her to walk with him to the foot bridge, she was ecstatic.

"I've got a biology exam, day after tomorrow, so I'll start cracking the books, tonight. Tomorrow, I'll study all night. Then the material will be fresh in my brain."

Elisa bit her tongue. Lucy Ann was taking the same exam. She had been studying for weeks.

That evening, Mrs. Carrots gave Lucy Ann permission to study as late as she wanted. Elisa was concerned. "Can you stay up two nights in a row?"

Lucy Ann twisted her mouth. "No. Why would I do that?"

"Well, the exam isn't until the day after tomorrow. Someone told me that you have to study all night, the night before an exam. Then the material's fresh in your brain."

Lucy Ann laughed. "That person's an idiot. Staying up all night before an exam is liable to turn your brain into mush. I've done it, so I know it's daft. When you're tired, you're likely to forget things and make stupid mistakes. It's much better to study ahead of time and go into an exam well rested. This exam may determine my entire future. The lads only need passing marks. I need to earn a First."

Elisa smiled proudly. "You will win a First. I'm sure of it."

"Thanks, Elisa. I'm pretty sure I will, too."

Later, Elisa lay half asleep, looking across the room at Lucy Ann's empty bed. Snuggling under her quilt, she remembered Colin walking her to the bridge. If he fancied her enough, they could elope to Gretna Green. She rolled over. No, she was too young. Chaps have gone to prison for taking girls to Gretna Green. Perhaps he'll talk to his father….

Per usual, the next day, Colin Edwards was the first to arrive for his art class. Elisa followed close behind. They politely greeted the art-master, then put on their smocks. Elisa knew she should stay silent until Colin initiated the conversation, but she was too excited. "Oh, Colin, it was lovely walking by the river, yesterday. The weather's even nicer, today."

Smiling indulgently, he spoke as if to a tiny child. "Pretty weather can't rule our lives, silly missy. Right after class, I have important studying to do. It's an all-nighter."

"No, you mustn't!"

He glared at her. "I beg your pardon?"

She clutched her hands, guiltily lowering her eyes. "I didn't mean... I'm sorry."

"Apology accepted." Turning away from her, he watched Robert setting out pastels.

Elisa's words burst out. "It's just that... Well, Lucy Ann's brilliant. All the masters say so. She says that studying all night, before an exam, can make you too tired, and you can make stupid mistakes."

Colin swung back to her. "How do you come to know Lucy Ann Minford?"

"She's my best friend."

Angry color rose in his cheeks. "Is she now!"

"She's been studying ever so hard. She says you lads only have to pass, but she has to earn a First. I don't think that's at all fair."

"She thinks she's getting a First?" Colin's chest heaved as he shook his finger. "No! No! No! She is *not* getting a first." He pulled off his smock. "Forgive me, Mr. Dennison, but I won't be taking class today. I have an exam, tomorrow."

Robert nodded his approval. "Understood, Edwards." Colin took his jacket and stormed out of the studio.

Elisa stood in shock. Colin may have been her only hope. She had driven him away, and she wanted to die. Tears welled in her eyes, then streamed down her cheeks. She ran out the door and the art-master called her back.

"Miss Roundtree!" She stopped and obediently turned to face him. "Do you have an exam tomorrow?"

She sobbed, "No, sir."

"Then come back to class, at once."

Hating the art-master, she swallowed her tears and went back to the studio. For the next miserable hour, she mindlessly toyed with colored pastels. A different Shakespeare sonnet ran over and over in her head,

Farewell, thou art too dear for my possessing...

She knew that Lucy Ann and Colin were both studying. She prayed, "Please God, let them both earn a First."

Two days later, Lucy Ann waited on boys' side for exam marks to be posted. She arrived back at Nicholas House, just as tea was being served. Mrs. Carrots and the girls stopped what they were doing. Lucy Ann stood, pursing her lips.

Mrs. Carrots scowled. "All right, child. Tell us how you did."

Lucy Ann broke into a smile.

Elisa shouted, "You made a First!"

"Yes!" Lucy Ann jumped up and down. "And second highest mark in the class." She hugged Mrs. Carrots and her house-mates, then ravenously crammed a sandwich into her mouth. "Dr. Theodore will have to let me continue for the rest of the year. Of course, I'll have to keep making Firsts."

Elisa hugged her, again. "You will. I know you will."

When the excitement quieted, Elisa sat next to Lucy Ann, whispering, "Did Colin Edwards make a First?"

Lucy Ann sputtered a laugh. "Edwards?" Elisa nodded and Lucy raised an eyebrow. "I wasn't even sure he'd get a passing mark. He did. He made a Third."

Chapter Twenty-three

Elisa always looked forward to the Autumn Festival and fancy dress ball. During the day, the girls wore their prettiest frocks, played croquet on the lawn, and flirted with the boys.

In the afternoon, they cheered boys playing cricket, and ate a delicious picnic on the lawn, accompanied by choral singing. Elisa was to solo with the girls' choir in Gilbert and Sullivan's *Climbing Over Rocky Mountains*. That night, everyone would wear costumes and dance at the ball.

Lucy Ann was dressing as a bookworm. She had made a giant mortar board, a huge pair of spectacles, and planned to wrap herself in a green sheet.

Pretty Meredith, Elisa's boring rival, was dressing as a princess.

Elisa would become Birnam Wood. She had sewn real leaves onto an old bathing costume, made a wreath of branches for her head, and a sign pointing to Dunsinane Hill. She prayed Colin Edwards would think she was amusing, but not too clever.

Elisa and Colin still met every afternoon in the art studio. He had barely spoken to her since his disastrous exam. Over and over, she replayed that horrible day. If only she had not spoken at all… if only… if only… Praying for his forgiveness, she smiled her sweetest smiles. Every day, he nodded politely, walked past, and ignored her. She promised herself to say nothing when she saw him today. She would look as pretty as possible, stare adoringly, and say absolutely *nothing*.

Carefully dressing in a pale-green frock with a tight bodice, leg of mutton sleeves, and a low rounded neck line, she was grateful bright sunshine streamed through their window. Even Lucy Ann had dressed in a stylish blue frock. Her long dark hair hung in a loose braid, instead of her usual severe knot. She stood behind Elisa, combing tangles from her hip-length copper mane.

Elisa sighed, "Oh Lucy, I know Collin is not as intelligent as you are, but he can still qualify as a doctor, can't he?"

Lucy Ann concentrated, working the comb through a tangle. "Well, yes. Sadly. His father will probably buy him a practice, whether or not he has any skill. I just hope he doesn't kill too many patients."

Elisa caught her breath. "Surely you're joking. I mean, well, doctors don't kill people. They cure them."

Lucy Ann twisted her mouth. "I sometimes wonder." She studied Elisa's hair, finally perfectly smooth and shimmering. "Do you want me to braid this, or pin it up? There seems to be no wind. You could risk wearing it loose. It looks so beautiful."

"Will Colin like it, do you think? I want to look pretty, but not immodest."

"Why hide your beauty? I wouldn't, if I had any." She pouted and Elisa spun around.

"You're very pretty Lucy. You just never let anyone see it. Your hair is beautiful too. Why not wear it long today?"

Lucy Ann thought for a moment, smiling. "No, better not. The moment I start looking too feminine, the headmaster will work even harder to toss me out of college. Why ever are you so keen on Colin Edwards? I know he's handsome, but he's a dull, insensitive lout. You deserve better."

Elisa longed to confide that she was already betrothed to a man far more objectionable than Colin. If she did, Lucy Ann would consider her married already, and never share another conversation about boys. She pretended to laugh. "Shall I keep looking, then?"

Lucy Ann shook her head. "You needn't look. Just stand still. They'll come to you."

Now Elisa laughed loudly, but her laugh was perilously close to tears.

Lucy Ann and Elisa were the last to leave Nicholas House. They hurried downstairs, and outside to Mrs. Carrots, busy in her sunflower garden. The housemistress waved. "You look lovely girls. Have a good time. I'll join you for the picnic." Since her gloved hands were black with digging in the soil, and dirt smudged her wrinkled face, they knew she was enjoying her free morning, and planned to stay away from the crowds as long as possible. The girls waved a cheery goodbye and hurried to join the festivities.

The playing field was surrounded by excited students, teachers and their families. Little children chased wildly after each other, adding to the festive atmosphere. Kitchen workers set up long tables for tea and sandwiches. Elisa chatted with her girlfriends, comparing frocks and hairstyles, all the while glancing around the field, looking for Colin.

She finally saw him, walking from the art studio. He carried a cricket bat and looked extra handsome in his white uniform. As he passed Nicholas House, Elisa scolded herself. He always painted on Saturday mornings. If she had stayed talking to Mrs. Carrots, he would have walked right past her. Instead, he marched down the field, toward pretty Meredith Locksley.

Elisa hurried to cut him off. "Hello, Colin." She smiled sweetly.

"Hello." He continued past and she followed.

"You finished painting early, today."

"Perhaps you haven't heard. There's a cricket match." He hurried toward Meredith.

Cheeks burning from his insult, Elisa turned and walked briskly back towards Nicholas House. She started to go into the house, then changed her mind, and walked to the studio.

Inside was as bright as outside, and deserted, except for Robert working in a corner. Elisa watched his back, fascinated to see how fast his brush moved from the colored paints on his pallet to the canvas on an easel, and back again. He looked very relaxed, painting a detailed street in a city she had never seen.

*

Imagining himself back on that delightful Paris street, Robert did not notice anyone had come into the studio. When he finally glanced up, he thought he was dreaming. Near the open doorway, framed in brilliant sunlight, stood a renaissance angel. The long copper halo of her lustrous hair shimmered around her beautiful face, over her slender shoulders and arms, curving gracefully at the full skirt of her immaculate, pale-green frock. His eager imagination saw her painted on canvass. Clothed or naked, she would be a perfect English rose in a class by herself.

All at once, he remembered that he was back in King Edward's England. It had been six months since he had enjoyed the company of a beautiful woman. He lived like a monk. The village near the school offered female companionship, but he was afraid of burly fathers with shotguns. The school grounds seemed to be dusted with desperate spinsters, or widowed school-mistresses chasing him with offers of home cooked meals or lace curtains for his cell-like room. He gently turned them all away.

He gazed at Elisa, thirstily drinking in her God given beauty. Since first seeing her on the train, he had been intrigued. She was so different from other girls. Didn't she know she was beautiful? Even today, dressed in an elegant frock, her extraordinary copper hair flowing loose over her shoulders, she showed no trace of vanity. He cleared his throat.

"Hmm, Hello, Miss Roundtree. Edwards just left."

She spoke through clenched teeth. "Thank you, Mr. Dennison. I know." She angrily tossed a smock over her frock, then tacked a piece of gray paper onto an easel. She grabbed a stick of charcoal, jammed it into the paper, and smashed it to bits.

Robert winced, but couldn't help smiling. Had she finally lost her patience with the young ass? He dragged his eager eyes away and stretched. "Everyone seems to be at the cricket match, Miss Roundtree, so I'm closing up shop. It's too nice a day to stay indoors." He hung up his smock.

"I *want* to stay indoors." She saw his painting, and walked closer. "Is that Paris?"

He smiled. "It is."

She stayed, admiring the half-finished canvas. "Do you miss it terribly?"

"Does it show?"

"Your manner, while you painted, you posture, the quickness of your brush strokes... You seemed very happy -- as if you were there." She moved closer, examining the canvas.

"Per usual, your observations are correct. I was very happy there. I never wanted to leave."

She spun around, "Why did you leave?"

"That -- is a long story." Smiling sadly, he dropped the oiled cloth cover over his canvas, pulled on his shirt cuffs and jacket, then waited by the opened door.

Elisa practically tore off her smock, flung it on a hook, and stomped outside. As she started toward the playing field, cheers and boos announced the start of the game. Robert locked the door, and started after her. She stopped. He stopped, watching her shoulders rise, then shudder.

She was crying. Suddenly, she made an about-face and ran past him, into the woods.

He watched her go, then looked back towards the sunflower garden. Mrs. Carrots was busy weeding. He didn't think she had seen him. Common sense told him to go to the cricket match and leave Elisa alone. His tender heart and throbbing loins sent him loping after her, into the forest. He found what seemed to be a path, through trees and briar. Before long, he spotted her hair shimmering like red-gold through the forest greens.

She was startled by a rustle behind her, turned, and leapt to her feet. He stumbled into a clearing. "So sorry, Miss Roundtree. I hope I didn't frighten you."

Feeling furious, but not daring to show it, she forced a smile. "Students are allowed to walk in the woods, Mr. Dennison. I apologize if there is a new rule that I have not yet learned...,"

He raised his hands. "No! No. You know the rules better than I do. I'm sure you're right. I just wanted...That is... Well...You were crying."

She lowered her eyes and forced her voice to stay low. "Forgive me, Mr. Dennison, I do beg your pardon. I never meant to trouble you. I shall go back...,"

"No, there's no trouble." He moved slowly towards her, as if gentling a nervous foal. "You were unhappy, that's all."

She glanced up suspiciously.

He stopped a few feet away. "You're a very pleasant person, and you are unhappy. I was concerned, nothing more."

He suspected that no upper-class gentleman had ever spoken kindly to her. His words sounded false. She closed her mouth and sat gracefully on a rock, perhaps hoping to bore him into leaving her alone.

His artist's eye blended the pale green of her frock, with the sparkling green of her eyes, and the surrounding dark green ferns. The sun glistened on her hair, and her cheeks glowed pink. She was absolutely delicious. He allowed himself a moment to drink in her beauty, then snapped back to reality. What the hell was he doing? If anyone saw him chase her into the woods, he'd be sacked, or worse. He should leave now, this instant. He started to go, then saw a tear roll down her cheek.

He took a step closer, smiling sympathetically. "It's none of my affair, but I couldn't help noticing the way Colin Edwards speaks to you. It's totally uncalled for, and you're right to speak your mind. He's a very dull chap. Not nearly good enough for you. Once you've finished school, you'll have a dozen suitors outside your door."

"I won't!" She sprang up. "Since you said I should speak my mind, I shall say that you know nothing of my circumstances and should not assume that you do."

He was bowled over. "I'm sorry, I never meant…,"

"I know you didn't mean…" She stiffened, reciting by rote: "Please forgive me. I am a foolish girl who must learn better manners. I promise never to speak out of turn, again." She cowered, holding her breath.

Robert stared. After a moment, he asked, "What dreadful person taught you to say that?"

Startled, she looked up.

He waited for an answer.

"My…," she swallowed. "My governess, when I was a child."

"Sure she wasn't a wicked stepmother?"

She smiled, uneasy. "You're not angry with me?"

"No. But, I am confused. You did that on the train."

"What did I do? I'm sorry if I did something wrong." The pain returned to her face.

"No, absolutely! You did nothing wrong." Frantic to reassure her, he smiled, motioning for her to sit. She perched stiffly on her rock. He crouched, none too comfortably, against a stump. "On the train, you stood up, as though you were going to be ill. All at once, you were fine."

She sat still as a porcelain doll. A vein pulsed lightly in her temple.

He guessed she was very upset, but afraid to show it. "Perhaps you weren't fine, after all. Perhaps you're just very good at hiding your feelings."

She stayed still. When he did not speak again, she whispered, "Men hate temperamental women. Men hate women who cry."

"I don't. Not when the tears are for a good reason. Everyone needs to cry, once in a while. I've done my share." He reached into his pocket and offered her his handkerchief.

She stared as though it were a foreign object. Moving closer, he took her hand and folded her fingers around the soft cloth. For the first time, she looked him in the eye. He smiled kindly and she caught her breath.

She took the handkerchief, and sniffed, "You're not at all like the other school-masters."

His delighted laugh revealed a row of white, even teeth. "Thank goodness for that."

She laughed with him and blew her nose.

He shook his head. "They're a frightfully boring lot. The only one I can abide is Jenkins. Do you know him?"

"I know who he is."

"Oh, right. You wouldn't be in his class. He teaches advanced sciences."

"My friend, Lucy Ann, is in his class. She's very intelligent."

"So are you."

She stared down at her hands.

"You are. You're one of my brightest students. You grasp concepts and implement them very quickly."

She twisted her mouth. "Perhaps in art. In math's…,"

"Do you like math's?"

"I hate it."

He chuckled. "Then it's sloth, not a lack of intellect."

She smiled shyly.

"I did well in school, but I never liked it. I could've gone to university, but I wanted to paint. Your talent is singing. I heard you in chapel. You were lovely. Aren't you singing a solo this afternoon?"

She nodded happily. "I love singing and playing the piano, but my real love is acting. Dramatics starts next week and I can't wait." She turned, suddenly excited. "Last spring we performed *Romeo and Juliet*. I played Juliet. It was wonderful. This time we're doing *The Taming of the Shrew*." Her smile was radiant. When he smiled back, she blushed, lowering her eyes. "You told us this is your first teaching position. Are you enjoying it?"

"More and more." His attention was pulled away as a bird swooped down to drink from the stream. "I just wish I could teach when I please and not all the time, because I have to."

Elisa's eyes went wide. "I thought grown men got to do as they pleased."

He sighed. "So did I… and I did what I pleased for almost eight years. When I was in Paris, I was poor as a church mouse, but I hadn't a care in the world. A few months ago my father died, leaving my mother with a mountain of debts. So here I am, slowly paying them off."

"That's terrible, about your father, and the rest. I'm so sorry."

He was flattered by her concern. "Teaching's not so bad. I enjoy you lot. It just leaves too little time for my own work."

Forgetting herself, she allowed a bright smile. "Your work is wonderful. I felt like I could walk down that Paris street, and the painting isn't even finished." She nervously twisted the handkerchief. " I only enrolled in your class to be near Colin Edwards, but now I like it, very much."

"You're very talented."

"Am I really?"

He nodded. She flushed with pride and he was thrilled to have made her happy. She relaxed, sliding off her hard rock, into a mass of ferns. The bodice of her frock pulled, emphasizing her slim waist and hips. Her small breasts pushed up against the stiff fabric. Robert stared, then looked away.

Elisa toyed with the handkerchief. "I like all your paintings. They're beautiful."

"Thank you. I hope the critics agree."

"What critics?" She looked up.

"I'm preparing an exhibit for London, next January. With luck, I'll sell some pictures, get some commissions, and then, I won't have to teach anymore."

Her smile faded. "Will you be leaving, then? After Christmas?"

"I wouldn't bet on it." Trying to ignore the urging of his loins, he crossed his legs, and leaned back on one elbow. "You needn't be concerned. You're in your last year. I'll surely be here that long. Perhaps we'll escape together."

She slowly lowered her eyes. "Escape?"

He chuckled, startling her. "I love that you're so comfortable on the ground. Most women worry more about their appearance than anything else."

She guiltily smoothed her skirt, now crushed, and slightly soiled. "I used to be a terrible tomboy. I never even wore frocks until I was ten."

He raised an eyebrow. "Your mother was very forward thinking."

"My mother died when I was born. I was brought up by my slightly dotty aunt, and servants who let me run wild. Our house is on the edge of the moors. I had a Shetland pony named Billy."

"I rode a pony named Billy, when I was a child."

"Really!" She giggled and sat up.

"Yes. It belonged to a neighbor."

"Pony Billy and I spent days roaming the moors. It was so wonderful. My clothes were a shambles, my hair a mess of knots." Embarrassed, she bit her lip. "I wore britches castoff from the stable boys."

He laughed, enchanted by her story.

"One day everything changed." Her arms pulled close to her body, making her thin frame appear even slighter.

Robert's heart beat with anticipation. "What happened?"

She nervously pulled her legs under her. "Oh, it's really of no account."

"It's of account to you. Please tell me."

She forced a giggle and stayed still. When he continued waiting, his face full of concern, she took a deep breath. "Well, one day a visitor came." Her eyes closed. "Sir -- John -- Garingham." She spoke the name with painful deliberation and Robert's eyes narrowed. "He wanted me to be a lady, so he took Billy away, and he brought a governess."

"The one who taught you that horrible apology?"

She nodded. "That apology's been very useful over the years. I'm always speaking out of turn. Sometimes I say that phrase and I don't get punished."

Robert shifted uncomfortably. "I take it, you get punished a lot."

Elisa stared at the ground.

"Does your father punish you?"

"Oh, yes." She sat up straight. "I'm sorry. This is a boring story."

"It's an unhappy story, but certainly not a boring one. Tell me more." He took off his suit jacket and carefully rolled it up for a pillow, then nestled against his tree stump, preparing to listen for a long time.

Elisa stared in disbelief. "Please forgive me. I've never had a proper conversation with a man. I'm not used to it."

Robert pushed thick dark hair off his high forehead, crossed his arms, and smiled. "You're doing fine. Please, go on."

She hesitated. "There's really nothing to tell. Sir John visits. Father hates me."

"Hates you? Why, for heaven sake? Is it because of your mother?"

"He's never spoken well of my mother, or me, or his sister, my Aunt Lillian. I don't know why he dislikes me, but he seems to dislike all women."

Robert shook his head. "I'll never understand blokes like that."

"The worst day of my life was my fourteenth birthday. Sir John cornered me in the pantry. His hands were... When I ran crying to my Aunt Lillian, she said, 'He's you're betrothed. He has the right.' I didn't believe her, so I asked Father. Soon after, I was sent to school. It was like heaven. I've been so happy here, I...,"

Robert lurched up. "You're betrothed to this man?"

"We're to be married in June."

"But you're too young, and you hate him."

"I'll be eighteen in December."

"Those bruises, on your wrist?"

"Sir John's always hurting me, but I'll never find another man. My aunt and Mrs. Carrots both say that a girl with no dowry must be grateful if *any* man wants to marry her."

"You must have a dowry."

"No, I assure you."

"This man didn't go to all the trouble of training you, and waiting all these years, if you have nothing to bring to a marriage."

She shrugged, nervously folding the handkerchief.

Robert was insistent. "Who told you, you have no dowry?"

"My aunt. She had none. That's why she never married and had to stay with her brother."

He shook his head. "There's something wrong with this story. Has no one...?"

The chapel bell rang, calling everyone to the picnic. Robert sprang up and helped Elisa to her feet.

"Shall I wash your handkerchief?" She dusted off her skirt. "I have to sing soon. I should have minded my frock."

Resisting the desire to take her in his arms, Robert took back the handkerchief. He gently pushed loose strands of copper hair away from her forehead. Her skin felt like warm porcelain under his fingers.

She smiled shyly, and seemed to enjoy his touch.

He whispered, "We mustn't be seen together. Shall I go back, first?"

"All right." She gazed into his eyes. "Thank you for listening to me. I hope I didn't...,"

"You're delightful. Thank you for sharing your story." Knowing he had to ravish her or walk away at once, he chose the latter, hurrying toward the insistent sound of the chapel bell. He stumbled from the woods, slightly dazed, confused, and wondering just exactly what had happened. Obviously, he had had a brief conversation with a pretty girl. That was nothing extraordinary. The fact that his heart was racing and his face burning was extraordinary.

Mrs. Carrots waved from underneath her tall sunflowers. He waved back and sprinted gracefully to her side. "Mrs. Carrots, you look a picture of health and beauty surrounded by your remarkable flowers."

She laughed at his compliment. "My flowers are doing very well this season. When I harvest their seeds, we'll feast on them all winter. Do you like sunflower seeds?" She raised an eyebrow. "You appear to be in excellent health, either that or you have a fever. I've never seen your color so high. Did you enjoy your walk in the woods?"

Robert paled. He didn't know what to say, but had to explain why he had followed an un-chaperoned female student into the forest. Before he was able to answer, he saw Elisa walk through the trees. Her pale green frock was almost a camouflage against the foliage, but her flowing red hair blew in the slight breeze. She looked like a fantastic wood nymph.

Elisa saw Mrs. Carrots with Robert, and stopped. Keeping her eyes low, she made her way tentatively towards them. Mrs. Carrots furiously pulled off her gloves and gathered her gardening tools into a sturdy basket. When Elisa reached the garden she couldn't help smiling at Robert. He couldn't help smiling back.

Mrs. Carrots glowered at them both. "Elisa, you heard the picnic bell. I believe you will be singing soon. You'd best hurry."

"Yes ma'am." She curtsied and hurried toward the picnic. Robert nodded to Mrs. Carrots and started after Elisa.

Mrs. Carrots barked, "Mr. Dennison!" He stopped dead. She spoke through clenched teeth, "Kindly help an old lady with her basket." She effortlessly lifted her basket of tools and thrust it at him. Looking very guilty, he took it from her and followed her into Nicholas House.

She pointed to a spot by the door. "The basket lives there." He obediently placed it on the floor and waited for her wrath. His momentary joy flipped to panic. He was sweating. His heart was beating out of his chest. Was this the end of his short career as an art-master? She had every right to report him to the headmaster and get him sacked. He braced himself for a verbal thrashing. Instead, she sighed deeply. Her eyes fill with tears. She blinked them away and pretended to look out the window.

She spoke softly, "Be careful, Mr. Dennison. This isn't Paris. It isn't even India, and that girl's fate is locked with cast-iron."

Robert whispered frantically, "But, it can't be. She told me she's betrothed to a sadist, of course she didn't use that word, but he hurts her. Her father is just as bad. She has no mother, only a useless aunt -- I saw her wrist, when she first arrived. God knows what that fiend will do once he's married to her. She has no idea what men...,"

"No, she hasn't, and it is not our place to educate her on such personal matters." Robert started to speak again, but Mrs. Carrots raised a finger to her lips. He was surprised when she chuckled and shook her head. "Actually, it's very funny. Elisa always insisted that I alone should know about her engagement. She even refuses to confide in her best friend, Lucy Ann Minford -- yet she seems to have told you everything in a few minutes." She wiped her eyes. "I agree with you, the situation is intolerable, and still we have no right to interfere."

Robert was frantic. "But there must be laws protecting...,"

"...Protecting penniless girls from marrying rich husbands? I think not."

"Is she truly penniless? It makes no sense...,"

"Her betrothed pays her tuition and spending allowance. If her family could afford the fees themselves...,"

"But surely she can get away...,"

Mrs. Carrots clenched her jaw and glared at him. "That child has slept under this roof for three years. I love her as my own. Do you honestly believe I haven't thought of everything? I've even thought of taking her back to India with me, but eventually, she'd be found and returned to her betrothed, leaving me to die in prison. Not a pretty picture, that."

Robert stood, stunned. "I hadn't thought of prison."

She waved a warning finger. "Do!" She washed her hands and face in the kitchen sink.

For a few moments, the only sound was water from the tap. Robert noticed a painting on the landing and moved close to study it. Far in the background stood the Taj Mahal. In the foreground, soft dust blew past the figure of a lithe woman in a green sari, a baby on her back. Mrs. Carrots turned off the tap. She looked sad as she dried her hands and face. Robert studied the paining. "The Sergeant Major had talent."

"He had."

"Your child?"

"Died from fever, soon after his father was killed in an ambush. That's why I left, and came to England."

"Do the girls know that woman is you?"

"Some do. Those who have asked. Elisa loves your class."

Torn between emotions, he nodded. "She's very talented. She learns so fast."

"Then, that must be your gift to her. If she is doomed to a lonely life in a loveless home, she will be able to create and enjoy art. You will have given her that. You should feel proud."

He rolled his eyes. "That is hardly enough."

"It must be. You can not do more." She moved to a mirror and straightened her hair. "And now, tell me, how are *your* pictures. Will they be ready for January?"

He nodded. "I'm pleased with the ones I have, but you're correct, and I need at least one portrait of a clothed model."

She looked sidewise at him.

"Please, may I paint Elissa?"

"It is pronounced, El-eez-a, and that is up to her." She faced him full on. "If she agrees, and I doubt she will not, for both your sakes, work only in the studio, or somewhere equally public. Never take her into the woods again."

"I didn't take her...,"

"I know, I saw. You followed her -- so don't follow her again -- and she roams there very often."

"Is she the girl who sneaks out at night?"

She threw up her hands. "Oh, dear God!"

149

"I shall never follow her into the woods again. I promise -- and we shall only be together in very public places."

"See that it's so." She hung up her smock, and gave herself a final once-over in the mirror. "Now, you may take my arm and walk me to the picnic. Everyone will think you are a chivalrous young man, kind enough to help an old lady. Make sure that is always what they think of you."

Robert bit his lip and bowed. "Yes ma'am. I shall do my very best."

Chapter Twenty-four

The next two weeks flew by as Elisa prepared her audition for *The Taming of the Shrew*. Robert allowed her to keep the script open on her easel and memorize while she drew. She quickly knew both principal roles, Kate and Bianca, by heart. Enjoying her excitement, he encouraged her to stay after class and practice her audition scenes. He was shy to read aloud, but she convinced him to read the other characters.

When the cast list was posted, Elisa read her name next to the character Kate, and screamed with joy. She pushed through boys and girls straining to read their names and raced to the studio. It was almost supper time, so the door was locked. On a chance, she ran through the woods, to the stream. Her heart leapt when she saw Robert sitting at a small easel, using pastels to capture autumn reds and golds.

"Mr. Dennison!"

He looked up and smiled at the youthful beauty rushing toward him. "What a pleasure, Miss Roundtree. Three times in one day." It was too late to remember his promise to Mrs. Carrots.

Elisa bubbled with excitement. "I've got Kate. I'm so excited. I was afraid Meredith Locksley would get the part, but she got Bianca. We start rehearsals tomorrow." Giggling, she dropped to her knees and looked up at him. "Everyone else thinks I'm silly, caring so much about a play, but unless we do another in the spring, this will be my very last play ever, so I have to be good."

He frowned. "Didn't you tell me you'd be living in Tebay, after you were married?" Elisa was startled and he quickly comforted her. "It's just that, I've been to Tebay. It's a big, wonderful seaside town. They're sure to have amateur theatrical societies."

"That may be so, but Sir John hates theatre and concerts." Her throat tightened. "He only lets me sing or recite when his guests ask me. He always says things like, 'We'll have none of that noise when your married to me,' and, 'You'll learn to be silent when you're married to me.'" She nervously bit her finger. "He hates it all. He hates me. I don't know why he wants to marry me." Her chin shook as tears filled her eyes.

"I'm so sorry." He reached to comfort her, then quickly sat back. "You were happy, and now I've made you cry. I feel like a cad."

She sniffed. "It's not your fault. There's nothing anyone can do. Women often marry against their will."

"Some women marry for love. Oh, my darling girl." He dropped down off his stool and cradled her in his arms.

Thrilled, she clung to him, looking up with sparkling green eyes. Without thinking, he turned his face and kissed her soft lips. She responded, pushing her body hard against his. He lurched back. "I shouldn't have done that." He jumped to his feet. "I'm terribly sorry."

A drop of rain fell on his cheek. They both looked up as a dark cloud drifted in front of the sun, releasing large droplets of water. He helped her to her feet. "You'll be a marvelous Kate. I can't wait to see you." He quickly packed up his kit and they both ran for cover.

Elisa hurried towards Nicholas House, but stopped when she saw Lucy Ann with five boys, laughing hysterically on the other side of the footbridge. Lucy Ann saw Elisa, and ran across. The boys ran in the opposite direction.

"Elisa!" Lucy Ann grabbed her arm as they ran through the rain toward Nicholas House. "You should have seen it. I made a dead frog jump from a dissecting dish. I thought Dr. Jenkins would have a fit."

By the time they reached their room, they were wet through and shivering. They quickly stripped down to nothing, wrapped themselves in warm robes, and combed out their long wet hair.

Elisa looked at her plain friend, still chuckling from the silly prank. "Lucy, you're so lucky. All the boys like you."

"They hate me when I make top marks." Lucy put a finger to her lips. She opened the door, peered out, closed the door, and tiptoed back.

Elisa made a face. "Whatever are you doing?"

"Shh," she whispered, "This is what we were really laughing about." She opened a heavy biology book, on her bed. "It's about reproduction."

"Of what?"

"Shh!! Of people."

Swifter than lightning, Elisa was next to her friend. Like guilty thieves, they huddled together and read through the chapter word by word. Lucy

Ann had it nearly memorized. Elisa was appalled. Was that what Sir John was talking about? Is that what he would teach her to do?

Lucy Ann closed the book, and put it on a shelf with a dozen others. "People like to do it, when they fall in love."

Elisa was still in shock. "Really?"

"Yes. It feels nice. My father's pharmacy shop is below our flat, and he comes home for lunch when we children are in school. We always know the days he and Mummy take a midday tumble, because they smile all through tea. They have seven children, so they must have done it a lot."

Both girls dissolved in giggles. Elisa looked at her plain friend, slightly prettier with her long hair strewn loose around her shoulders. "You're with boys all the time, Lucy Ann. How is it you never fall in love?"

Lucy Ann rolled her eyes. "I want to be a doctor, Elisa, to go to university. I don't have time for..." Suddenly embarrassed, she grabbed a comb and violently pulled it through her hair.

Elisa's mouth dropped open. "Lucy! Are you in love with someone?"

She ripped out a rat's nest. "Your trouble is you're too pretty. Boys are afraid of you."

"Mr. Dennison isn't afraid of me."

Shocked, Lucy Ann stopped. "The art-master?"

Elisa looked away and started combing her hair.

Lucy Ann whispered frantically, "Surely, you're not as daft as that? If it were even suspected that you fancied each other, you'd be expelled. He'd be let go without a reference. He'd never find another position. Not ever."

There was a knock on the door. A girl handed in four letters.

"Thanks, Molly." Elisa took the letters as the girl continued down the hall. "Here Lucy. Three for you."

Lucy Ann took her letters. "I'm serious."

"I'm not." Elisa forced a laugh. "I was joking. Why ever would a grown man fancy a silly schoolgirl?" Turning away, she lay face down on her bed, and tore open her pink envelope. Lucy Ann watched her, then sat down to read her own mail. Elisa smoothed out the pages and dutifully plowed through her aunt's almanac of village gossip. After tedious listings of who had jilted whom, which apples were best this season and who's cow had died, Lillian had added a postscript.

153

"…You must promise not to say I told you, but a wonderful Christmas surprise is planned. On your birthday, December 23rd, you are to be married. Your father has decided that it is foolish to wait until the end of the school year. Sir John is very happy and has booked passage to Paris for your honeymoon. Oh, my darling, I am so happy for you!"

*

Robert sat in his room, counting out pocket change. Scowling, he placed his coins on the wash stand. No visits to the village pub this month. He had to sell some paintings. With only his salary, his father's debts might never be paid off. Muffled voices sounded from the masters' common room, downstairs. Robert hoped Dr. Jenkins had returned, or Monsieur LeGrand. The French-master was a dull chap, but Robert wanted to practice his fading French. It was still light outside, but the stairwell was quite dark. Leaving his door open, Robert walked down the four flights, passing the steward.

"Good evening, Mr. Longworth."

Flattered at being addressed as "Mister," Longworth held up his lighted taper. "And a very good evening to you, sir." He lit a wall sconce and continued up to the next floor.

When Robert reached the common room, an inviting fire blazed in the hearth. He was disappointed to see only Canterville and Hargrave reliving an ancient cricket victory. When they tried to involve Robert in their debate, he pleaded fatigue, selected a book from the ample selection, and climbed back to his room. He lit a candle on his rickety bedside table, added coals to his small stove, then closed the door and changed into his night clothes. He climbed under the bedclothes, pushed the pillow behind his back, and read. The novel was not to his liking, so after a few pages, he exchanged it for a sketch pad and pastel sticks.

He marked one end of the paper with red and black curves, creating a voluptuous, dark-haired beauty. *Oh, Margot, I wonder who's sharing your warm bed tonight.* As he drew the rounded shape of her full buttocks and thighs, the memory of her solid flesh sent his pulse racing. He turned the page around, choosing lighter colors, and a luscious blue-eyed blond appeared. *Dear Sonja, Are you still trying to marry the count?* He felt his hands caressing her large soft breasts as their creamy skin tones appeared from the chalk between his fingers.

154

Robert turned the page lengthwise, changing to earth tones, and a slender nymphet danced between the mature women. His heart pounded with guilt and excitement. *How do I pronounce her name? Elissa? Eliza?* His fingers flew, coloring her soft young nipples the same rosebud pink of her lips. His mouth ached to suck those sweet, firm virgin breasts. The bright triangle of hair between her slender hips shone the same copper as the luxurious mane, falling past her waist. He imagined his fingers exploring the baby soft folds of skin between her legs. *There you are, Elly. My sensuous little nymphet.* As the fingers of his left hand clutched the pad, the fingers of his right hand slid under the bedclothes. He closed his eyes. *Oh, My darling Elly. Oh, yes! Yes!*

Chapter Twenty-five

The storm continued. Overnight, the weather changed. A gloriously warm autumn was howled away by rain and wind. After Lucy Ann fell asleep, Elisa lay in bed, looking out the window, watching fiercely colored leaves cling to shaking branches. Those leaves were warring against winter. She was warring against her father. They would all lose. Her insides churned, ready to explode with anger and frustration.

She whispered to the faint crescent moon. "I was meant for something, surely. No creature is placed on this earth for nothing. Who am I, where do I belong? I know I have a soul because it's crying out to me now. It's reaching for something, someone, I don't know what, but I must find something to hold, to love, to give to, and be nourished by. My heart is filled with nameless longings. I long for... I long for..." She fell into a troubled sleep.

She woke at dawn. Knowing Robert liked early morning light, she wrapped a coat around her nightdress, climbed down the trellis and went to the studio. He was lacquering a painting modeled from pastels he had made by the river. She clapped her hands. "It's wonderful. I can almost smell the river. It's perfect!"

He laughed. "Oh, no, my dear. If it were perfect I'd have no reason to go on living."

She laughed. "How silly! You don't mean that."

"I do mean it. Strange as it may seem, pretty one, this...," he made a grand gesture around the four walls, "is my whole life."

She looked around, suddenly serious. "No, it's not strange. I understand."

Throughout the day she thought about what Robert had said. His whole life was art. She wished her whole life could be the theatre. Her happiest hours had always been performing on stage, or watching a theatrical event. The highlight of every summer was the arrival of the London touring companies. Her Aunt Lillian loved the theatre and took her to see many wonderful plays. She would never forget Simon Camden's *Hamlet* and Jeremy O'Connell's *Henry V*. Of course, women who made their living on the stage were harlots and shunned by polite society. But, well-bred ladies were expected to join amateur theatricals and entertain their friends, at home. If only Sir John would let her do that, she might endure anything else.

A few days later, she paid Robert Dennison another early morning visit. He was working at an easel and did not hear her come in. As soon as he saw her, he pulled an oiled cloth over the painting and spun to face her. "Good morning, Miss Roundtree." He stood in front of his easel, guarding it like a sentry.

She stopped in her tracks. "Good morning, sir." She knew she was intruding, but craned her neck, trying to see what he was hiding. "Please," she swallowed. "May I see your painting?" He hesitated, then pulled back the cloth. It was a naked woman drying herself from a bath. The woman glanced casually over her shoulder, as if she were watching the painter. She looked serene and comfortable.

Elisa caught her breath and tried not to look shocked. "She's so beautiful."

"Yes, she is beautiful."

"Who is she?"

"A model." He pulled the cloth back down.

Elisa swallowed. "I'd better get back before they miss me." She knew her cheeks were pink.

"See you later, then." He smiled as she ran from the room.

A few days later, she sneaked out early, once again. Used to her daybreak visits, Robert barely glanced up from his tiny canvas.

"Good morning." He paused, then stared at his painting. "Come over here, will you?"

She went over and looked at the canvas. It contained a single red-gold leaf. He took a piece of her hair and held it up to the painting. They both laughed. The leaf was that exact color. He shook his head. "That red-gold has been haunting me. I spent an hour mixing and re-mixing. I thought I was going mad... and," he paused, still holding her hair. "Here's the reason why." He smoothed the hair over her shoulder. "So one mystery is solved."

"Are there others?"

He rolled his eyes, chuckling sadly. "Life itself is a mystery, my dear." He went back to work.

"Please go on."

He gave her a comical look. "Do you want me to wax philosophical this morning?"

"Yes, please."

He looked slightly embarrassed. "I can't say anything profound, Miss Roundtree. I only know that every morning is a wonder, sometimes of delight, sometimes of horror. We search every day, craving approval, longing for peace, crying for affection, and usually settling for far less than our ideal."

Her throat tightened. "But, must we always settle? Must life be that hard?" Starting to cry, she covered her mouth and turned away.

"I don't know." He sadly set down his brush. "I wish there was something I could do for you. I feel so helpless."

"You help me every day. Really! You mustn't feel otherwise. You're the best friend I've ever had."

"That can't be true."

"It is. You let me say whatever I please, even when it's nonsense."

"You never speak nonsense." He stepped toward Elisa and she smiled hopefully. Remembering himself, he turned back to his canvas.

She hesitated. "Do you want to paint me?"

He caught his breath. "Um... Yes. Yes, Elly. I would love to paint you."

She smiled. "Elly?"

He blushed. "I'm sorry Miss Roundtree, but I can't pronounce your name."

She felt her cheeks warm. "My mother gave me a German name no one can pronounce, but no one's ever called me 'Elly.' I like it."

Keeping his eyes on her, he shook his head. "Well, all right then -- Elly. When we're in private, my name is Robert. Rob, to my chums."

The chapel bell rang. Elisa sighed and turned to go. "Oh, by the way... Robert."

He looked up.

"I've had a letter from my aunt." Her lower lip trembled. The words burst out. "I'm to be married at Christmas." She ran from the studio.

*

Eight weeks remained before the end of the school term, and the date Robert's pictures were due in London. Although on schedule with his

158

preparations, he was still anxious. After eight years as a starving artist, this exhibit could change his life. He needed everything to be perfect. Morning and night, he worked feverishly, finishing some canvases and remounting others. He felt his collection was unbalanced, but the thought of starting a new painting this late, had been unthinkable. Now that Elisa had offered herself as his model, it seemed possible.

One early morning she raced into the studio. "Oh, Robert! Last night's rehearsal was brilliant. We finished staging the play. When I recited Kate's last speech, I really felt I was in love with Petruchio. I wanted to serve him. I wanted '*my hand... to do him ease*' because I loved him, not because I had to." She paused. "I think a woman should *want* to obey her husband. Don't you?"

He raised his eyebrows. "I don't think anyone should *want* to obey anyone. If I ever marry, which is doubtful on my wages, I want my wife to be a partner, not a servant."

She stood still, digesting the idea. "But... partners are equals. I can't even imagine being a man's... partner." Her brows pulled together in a worried frown. "Sir John certainly doesn't want a partner. He said that he would tame me, that he would teach me to obey. When I said that I already obeyed him and he already did everything he wanted, he laughed and said that I was an 'innocent.' He said he would teach me to do things I had never even thought of."

Robert nearly dropped his palette. She reached to catch it and they lifted it together. Their fingers touched. They both glanced out the windows. Across the river, three masters walked together. No one was out on the girls' side.

Robert took the palette from her. "Oh dear, you've got paint on your fingers." She happily let him wipe her hand with a clean rag. The chapel bell rang, but he kept holding her hand.

She playfully squeezed his fingers. "It's time for me to go."

He smiled, pulling away. "We'll talk later."

"We can never talk when the other students are here." She looked very sad.

His insides churned. "Go on. You'll be late." He was dying to take her in his arms, but he stayed still.

She sighed sadly, turned and left the studio.

He picked up his brush and palette, muttering to himself, "She's in for a worse life than she even imagines. What sort of man is he? I can't believe her delightful energy is going to be locked away into a sadistic marriage of convenience. If I had money, I'd carry her out of here this instant. I'd hire the best lawyers in London, and free her from whatever hold that monster has over her father. There's got to be a way to free her. Any life would be better than that."

He made himself concentrate. Choosing a yellow-green on the palette, he touched it with the tip of his brush and gently stroked it across the canvas. "She's so happy on the stage. If only…" Struck with a thought, he stood back. "I just got a letter from Mike. Why not ask him?" He put down his brush and palette, and covered his painting. Dashing back to his room, he wrote a letter to His Majesty's Theatre.

Chapter Twenty-six

After a late rehearsal, Elisa raced to Nicholas House, exhausted and happy. She exchanged a few words with Lucy Ann, before snuggling into the bedclothes and drifting into a deep sleep. Tossing fitfully, she dreamed of her young Petrucio's boyish face. "...*Thou must be married to no man but me...*" The boy transformed into Garingham beating her with Miss Kimball's switch. "Elisa!" he scowled, showing yellow teeth. She pulled away with all her might, but couldn't move. The boy reappeared in front of her. "...*For I am he am born to tame you Kate.*" His slight frame broadened into middle-aged girth. The schoolboy blazer faded into a dark gray suit and the boy's pretend frown became Garingham's glower. He dragged her screaming down dark stone steps into a dungeon. "You are my wife and you will obey!"

Elisa lurched awake, gasping for breath, and drenched with sweat. Her heart pounded as she threw off the bedclothes. After a few moments, she lay back. Silent tears soaked her pillow. The rain had stopped. Bright moonlight flooded the room. Careful not to wake Lucy Ann, she tiptoed to the window, pushed it open, and inhaled deliciously clean, fragrant air. Huge stars seemed to be trapped in the tops of trees.

Checking the time, she was amazed to see that it was three o'clock. She had never been awake at this hour. The entire school was asleep. If she went out now, she could be totally alone. She slipped on a coat and rubber boots, then climbed out the window and down the trellis. Once on the ground she shivered. Her grotto would be soaking wet, so she walked along the river.

There was a light in the art studio. Peering in a window, she saw that the room was cluttered with pictures. Robert moved pictures from place to place. One table was covered with pastels, another with watercolors, and the largest area with oils.

She understood why Robert was always tired. He could only prepare his exhibit when the studio was empty. If she were his partner, she could help him right now, go to London with him, and be with him at his exhibit. She shivered and hurried back to her warm bed. She dove under the bedclothes and beat her fist against the pillow. "When his exhibit opens, I'll be married. I may as well be dead."

Robert had deep circles under his eyes. Lack of sleep and worry about his London show left him unusually short tempered. Elisa was elbow deep in gray clay, molding a figure of her character, Kate. Robert made his rounds of the other students, then moved close to her. Pretending to help her with a tool, he whispered, "Stay after, we need to talk."

When the chapel bell rang, Elisa took her time, letting the other students go ahead of her, washing their hands at the cold water taps. She was still rinsing gray clay from under her fingernails, when the last student left.

Robert collected supplies forgotten by the students. Looking out a window, he saw Lucy Ann and some other girls tossing a large ball. One girl missed the catch, and the ball rolled underneath the window. Lucy Ann ran to fetch it. Seeing Robert and Elisa inside, she waved through the glass. They waved back. She tossed the ball to her friends, and motioned that Elisa should come and join them.

Elisa shook her head and smiled at Robert. "Lucy thinks I'll get into trouble, spending so much time with you." She busied herself, gathering supplies. Lucy Ann wagged a scolding finger, then went back to her game.

Robert watched her go and spoke softly. "She may be right. Listen, I've done some inquiring. Do you know Miss Bennett, from the accounting office?"

Elisa nodded, her eyes wide.

He curled his lip. "She fancies me."

Picturing the bossy woman with small eyes and spectacles, Elisa giggled.

"I'm afraid I misused her good will. I asked her to go through your records and see who was paying your tuition. It's been Sir John Garingham, the entire four years."

"I told you that."

"I just wanted to make sure. Now that I *am* sure, I am also sure, that you must be the heiress to an estate. Since the man is obviously not spending his money for love, he must expect a healthy return on his investment. That investment being you."

Elisa shivered. "But, if there is an estate, my father controls it."

"Not necessarily. Your mother was German. There may be European holdings he can't touch. I've been wracking my brain, but there's no way I can find out anything by myself. Once I'm in London…,"

"I'll already be married."

"Maybe not."

"But I showed you my aunt's letter."

"Yes, and you told me half-a-dozen fantasies she's invented. She's the one who says you have no dowry. No one else. You told me Sir John hates traveling."

"That's right. He says he'll never go anywhere again, where they don't speak English."

"So he's taking you to Paris? In January? No one goes to Paris in January. It's dreary. I know."

Elisa's brows pulled together. "Aunt Lillian always wanted to go to Paris."

"And she always wanted to get married. Is it possible…?"

"That she's making it up?" She shrugged, suddenly hopeful. "Last year Sir John said there was to be no honeymoon at all. After the June wedding, he was just going to take me to his house in Tebay. My aunt cried for days. If she has made it up, it gives me more time, but still…,"

He moved closer. "You have enough time to get away."

"Away from where?"

"From anywhere your father could find you."

Elisa paled. "What are you talking about?"

Robert went into a storage cupboard, reached behind a pile of drawing pads and pulled out a letter. "I need to discuss this with you, but we can't be seen reading it together." He slipped the letter inside his coat pocket. "It's time I was locking up." He thought for a moment then angrily slammed the cupboard door. "Is there no place we can have privacy?"

Elisa paused in thought. "I know a place, but you might not like it."

"I'll like it. Take me there." They grabbed their coats and left the studio.

The late afternoon sun was bright as Elisa led the way, taking them deep into the woods. Robert cursed himself. So much for his promise to Amelia Carrots. He was really risking the sack this time, and he'd deserve it. Elisa stopped, waiting for him to catch up. She pushed apart two bushes, crouched down and climbed through the narrow opening.

Robert followed and smiled, taking in the tiny shelter. The forest floor was fragrant with prickly pine needles and honeyed heather. An almost perfect canopy of branches and giant ferns sheltered them from the wind. It was surprisingly warm.

Wobbling on his haunches, he took off his coat, spread it over the ground, and lay on top of it. Elisa's shyly stretched out next to him. Without hesitation, he took her in his arms, pulled her close, and kissed her. She was startled and delighted. He sat up. "Sorry – That's not why we're here."

Her hair had come loose, tangling with leaves and pine needles. Dappled light poured through the leafy covering. "Wait! Don't move. I think I see how I'm going to paint you." He arranged her hair so it framed her like a halo. Turning her face in different directions, he made patterns of light reflect across her pale skin. Finally satisfied, he smiled. "That's it. That's my Autumn Lady."

She blushed. "I must look like a witch."

"You do. You're utterly enchanting." They both laughed. He noticed the letter, now a crumpled mess, sticking from his inside coat pocket. He smoothed it over his knee. "I wrote a school chum, Michael Burns. He's an actor. He toured for a long time and he's done well. For the past two years he's been at His Majesty's Theatre, in London. I'll be staying with him while I'm there."

"How long will you be away?"

"If all goes badly, only the five days of the show. If all goes well...," he raised his eyes to heaven, "...forever. I told Mike about you, asking how one gets started on the stage. This is his answer." He offered her the letter and she stared as if it were poison. "Elly, if we don't do something quickly, you're doomed to marry into a lifetime of hell."

"I know that. I tried to find another man to marry me. I thought one of the students..." She shook her head. "Colin was my last chance."

Robert shuddered. "Colin Edwards hates women as much as Sir John Garingham. No *man* can save you. You're seventeen, your father wants you to marry Garingham and he'll never let you marry anyone else. You've got to save *yourself*." He held out the letter. "Here's a chance to get away – away from everything that you hate, and to do something that you love."

She sat up, appalled by the idea. "But, I couldn't go on the stage. Everyone knows what actresses are. They're…" Unwilling to say a bad word, she pursed her lips.

"That's ridiculous. Most people think that painters are…" Looking at the vulnerable virgin in front of him, he held his tongue, fumbled with nervous fingers, and half tore the envelope as he pulled out the letter. He flipped to the third page and read aloud.

"…I've made some inquiries pertaining to your young lady. I can't wait to meet her. She may be in luck. In the spring, a new production of THE TEMPEST is planned. Herbert Beerbohm Tree's acting company is touring America. Our resident actor-manager is looking to cast one really beautiful girl to be some sort of fairy shadow to appear throughout. She'll have no lines and he plans to hire a 'super' just for the one production. I told him about your girl. He doesn't need another apprentice, but said he could take one on. Apprentices receive no wages and are overworked. They do get free lodgings and wretched food in a horribly dirty boarding house. They also get the best training available, acting classes taught by Jeremy O'Connell. Some top actors and actresses have worked their way up through the ranks. If your young lady is as beautiful as you say, and if this sounds appealing to her, auditions will probably be on December 18th, the day after MACBETH opens. Let me know if she's interested, and I'll find out more details.*

Write soon, Rob, and tell me what I can do to facilitate your triumph. I hope you can stay longer than just the week. We'll have tremendous fun!

Yours Ever,
Mike"

Elisa's eyes were huge. "Acting classes are taught by Jeremy O'Connell?"

Puzzled, Robert folded the letter into the envelope. "Do you know him?"

She huffed. "Of course I don't *know* him. He's a famous actor. Respectable people don't socialize with people of his sort. Aunt Lillian takes me to see the touring companies in Skipton. We saw him on stage. I would never, 'know him.'" She thought for a moment. "And, I could never go to London. The very idea is ridiculous."

"Why? All you need is the train fare."

She shrugged in despair. "Who would go with me? I can't travel without a chaperone."

"You traveled here by yourself."

"Only this one time. Auntie always came with me, before. I've never been anywhere, alone."

"You'll only be alone during the journey. Michael will meet you in London. He's a delightful chap."

"I should meet a strange man, in a train station? No thank you!" She crossed her arms and scowled.

"You'd rather go to Tebay and marry Sir John Garingham?"

"You know I'd rather die, but December 18th is in the middle of the Christmas holiday. I've no means to get away from home."

"Then don't go home. Stay here. Some students always stay over the hol's, or so I'm told. I'll be staying, along with your Mrs. Carrots."

"You're not going home?"

"I can't afford it. I'm saving every penny for London. Working the holiday will cover my days away in January and I won't be docked any pay. I don't even have to teach, just stay in residence and look after the boys."

Thinking hard, she bit her lip. "If I did audition, and they did take me, I'd be in London when you arrive."

He smiled at her bright eyes, shining green against the foliage. "I thought of that. It would be wonderful, but my circumstances mustn't influence your decision."

"What if they don't take me?"

"Then you can come back. Provided you've got the train fare. Do you have any money?"

"I never use my spending money. I've saved a few pounds."

"A few *pounds*? Goodness, you're better off than I am. But do you want to come back at all? Perhaps you can audition for other theatres, or find some other employment... as a telephone operator, or shop girl, or a music teacher, anything to keep you hidden until we can clear the mystery of your inheritance. There are very respectable boarding houses for young ladies."

Her eyes grew huge. "Could I get a position and support myself? I've read stories about girls...,"

"Of course. With your beauty and manners, there are a dozen things you can do. You're clever enough to learn one of those new typewriting machines." She looked frightened and he took her in his arms. "I know. It's a lot to think about."

Shivering, she pulled in her legs and curled up, nestling against his chest.

He kissed the top of her head. "You don't need to decide now. Sleep on it. Play make-believe. Imagine the possibilities." He rocked her like a baby. "Before I start a painting, I have to have a detailed picture in my mind. If I don't see the image in my mind beforehand, it won't come out on the canvas. Go home, rest, and try to imagine what your life can be like. In a day or two, tell me what you've seen.

Elisa seemed so comfortable, cradled in his arms, he never wanted to move. The musty aroma of the damp forest was intoxicating. He closed his eyes and kissed her sweet mouth. She shivered as he opened the buttons of her coat and slid his fingers inside. Very lightly, he caressed her breasts, stroking and squeezing. Even through layers of fabric, he felt her body tense. Very slowly, he slid his hand under her skirt. She jerked back, but he held her tight.

"It's all right. Just relax. You'll like this."

She stared with frightened eyes. "What are you doing?"

He whispered. "You've liked what I've done so far. You know I'd never hurt you." She trembled and he held her tighter. "Just relax. Trust me."

She closed her eyes. He kissed her again, and slid his fingers up between her legs. She gasped as he began rubbing, first gently, then harder, until she groaned with pleasure, clamping her legs together like a vice. Her entire body pulsed. She clung to him as if she were drowning. After a minute, her heart calmed. She collapsed like a rag doll. He held her tight. She felt safe.

His erection stabbed painfully and he was tempted to take her right then. Suddenly, Mrs. Carrot's warning echoed in his head. *What am I doing? I'll be jailed for a rapist.* He pushed as far back as the small enclosure allowed.

Elisa gazed up with trusting eyes. "When will you start painting my portrait?"

He pulled his jacket over the painful bulge in his trousers. "Now that I see it in my mind, we can start tomorrow. It's late. You'd better go." When she stayed, he gently nudged her. "Go on."

She obeyed, staggering from the grotto, into the chilly wind.

The second she was gone, Robert ripped open his trousers, relieving himself on a fern.

*

Mrs. Carrots was surprised to receive a letter from Anthony Roundtree. She called up the stairs. "Elisa!"

"Yes, Mrs. Carrots?" Elisa came downstairs.

"Your father seems to be writing about a different daughter than the one I know. He's suddenly concerned about your studies. Any idea why?"

Elisa shrugged and took the letter. Reading the lines, her resolve to run away became stronger than ever.

Dear Mrs. Carrots,

My daughter has requested that she be allowed to remain at school over the Christmas holiday and continue her studies. I find this to be a reasonable request, and readily agree that she should stay. You may be aware that she is to be married in June. Despite the efforts of fine governesses and your admirable school, she refuses to learn the most elementary courtesies a young lady must acquire in order to become a proper wife. Perhaps intensive tutelage can finally make a difference. Since her fiancé does not plan to visit this winter, I see no need for Elisa to come home.

Yours Respectfully,
Anthony Roundtree

Elisa handed back the letter and tried not to smile. Robert was right. Her Aunt Lillian had invented the Paris honeymoon.

Mrs. Carrots raised an eyebrow. "Well, my dear, you don't seem a bit unhappy. You usually enjoy holidays at home when your betrothed is not present, yet you seem very pleased to stay at school. Do you want to tell me why?"

The girl's eyes widened as she searched for a plausible story.

"Come, child. You've no talent for lying. Tell me the truth."

"Well… Um… You know that I love it here."

"Even so…,"

"I've only got until the spring. After that…" Not knowing what else to say, she started to cry.

"All right, child. Don't upset yourself. Whatever it is, I'm pleased you'll be joining us." She raised an eyebrow. "I'm sure Mr. Dennison will be pleased, as well."

Elisa paled. "He won't care. He'll have finished painting my portrait."

"And that's his only interest in you?"

"Of course." Her cheeks flushed. "What else could it be?"

"What else, indeed?" The school mistress rolled her eyes and continued in a businesslike fashion. "Well, the play is two weeks from Friday. Some students will be leaving directly after. On Saturday, when the rest go home, the few of us that are staying will move to boys' side, into Rogers House. It's the biggest. We women will take the second floor and the boys will take the third and fourth floors. Mr. Dennison will take the house-master's suite on the ground floor. He suggested that I take the suite, but it's filled with the house-master's personal belongings, so I prefer to stay in a student room. Pack only a few items. You can leave the rest here."

Chapter Twenty-seven

"Elly darling, please! You must sit still. I'm almost done."

"I'm sorry, Robert." Elisa sat shivering in a low backed chair on the model's platform. Cold morning sunlight struggled through thick clouds. She clutched her hands in her lap. "I love posing as your *Autumn Lady*, but had no idea it was going to be this hard. We rehearsed until late. I barely slept." She yawned and he scowled.

"You volunteered for this, remember. You weren't conscripted. Just think lovely thoughts."

She giggled sleepily. "Looking at you is everything lovely in the world."

He laughed and shook his head. "Silly twit."

She giggled some more, her mind racing with the coming events. The play was in three days. In ten days, she was to audition at His Majesty's Theatre. In between, she and Robert would be sleeping under the same roof. The memory of their tryst in the grotto was like a never ending hunger. Will he ever touch her like that again? The aching desire between her legs was like a gnawing pain with no hope of relief.

Since that tryst, they had spent every available moment as artist and model, in the very public studio. He worked every night, putting finishing touches on his pictures: varnishing, backing, finally packing them for shipment. Now, behind his easel, the brush in Robert's hands seemed to have a life of its own. He had never worked so fast or so well. He had painted dozens of portraits, but this one seemed to paint itself.

He was amused by the vision on the canvas. While definitely Elisa, it was an Elisa of the future, the way she might look in five years, when the lithe nymphet grew into sensual maturity. *I wonder if I'll be around to see her. In five years she'll probably be married with a brood of kids.* Like the crash of a cymbal, his vision was gone. The magic left the brush. He pulled it away before it could spoil the perfect canvas. Stepping back, he took a deep breath, put down the brush and palette, and rubbed his sore eyes. *You stupid ass. It was going so well. You've got the concentration of a flea.*

Elisa gasped. "I'm so sorry. I'll stay still. I promise."

He leaned back, exhausted. "It's not you, my angel. You were perfect." He wiped his stained fingers on a cloth. "You've been wonderful, really. You're as tired as I am. I can finish without you. You don't need to pose again."

She was very relieved.

*

Cheers and applause filled the great hall as the cast of young actors held hands, bowing again and again. Bittersweet tears ran down Elisa's cheeks as the final curtain fell, shuddered, and stayed still. All at once, she was hugged by a half-dozen fellow thespians. Most had families in the audience and were traveling home that night. When the stage cleared, Elisa was the last to leave. Unwilling to take off her costume, she hung back, talking to anyone who would listen.

Finally, the teacher acting as costume mistress, called her. She went to the dressing room, slipped off the heavy blue gown and headdress, then watched tearfully as they were packed away into a trunk. Will she ever get to wear another costume? *Yes!* She clenched her jaw. Next week she will be at a real theatre. They must take her. *They must!* Real actresses must love acting as much as she did. Surely they were not all harlots. If they were, their lives must still be better than her own. Leaving on her makeup, she dressed and hurried out, into the frigid night air.

Lucy Ann waited, shivering, holding a small box. "Finally!" She hugged her friend. "You were fabulous."

Elisa smiled gratefully. "Thanks Lucy. Is that for me?"

Lucy Ann scowled. "Mr. Dennison asked me to give it to you."

She looked around frantically. "Where is he?"

"He left."

Elisa quickly opened the box. Carefully wrapped in tissue paper, was a figurine.

Lucy Ann stared. "It's you!"

Elisa stared as well, turning the piece over and over. "It *is* me. It's Kate. It's perfect. How did he know what my costume looked like?" Four inches tall, the figure was a perfect likeness of Elisa. Robert had captured the tones of her skin and hair, the tilt of her face and the lean of her slender frame.

"Here's a note." Lucy Ann pulled a card from the bottom of the box and read,

"Dear Miss Roundtree,
I hope you don't mind my finishing your figurine.
You were too busy to complete her, and she was too good
a piece to throw out.
R. Dennison"

Elisa took the card. "Whenever did he find the time?"

Lucy Ann huffed, "Right. He's spent all his time painting you." She re-wrapped the tiny statue. "I'm glad that's over. I was afraid you'd get yourself into trouble." She took Elisa's arm, and the girls walked to Nicholas House.

Elisa held the box against her heart. *I don't want any trouble… But I love you Robert. I'll do anything to be with you.*

*

The houses on the boy's side were larger than the houses on girls' side. Saturday evening, Elisa wandered around Rogers House, finding wonderful nooks and corners filled with surprising things. Where she was used to finding piles of embroidery, she found cricket bats and balls. Crochet hooks were replaced by woodworking tools and half-finished model sailboats stood by a window. Being a boy seemed like fun.

Determined to give the children a real holiday, Mrs. Carrots had a Christmas tree brought in. She took Elisa and a lively nine-year-old named Sarah to stay with her on the second floor. Robert took the ground-floor master's suite and the boys went to the third and fourth floors. With all the running up and down stairs, it was very noisy.

The master and students usually living in the house had left it very untidy. Sunday, when the maid-of-all-work arrived, she found piles of dirty bed linen, floors caked with grit, and towers of dirty dishes in the kitchen. Monday morning, Mrs. Carrots realized that one maid could not keep up with the volume of housekeeping, and assigned everyone chores. The house was scrubbed from top to bottom. When the children were finally settled into their clean, temporary rooms, Mrs. Carrots assigned school hours. Elisa was so nervous about her trip to London, she was actually happy to divert herself with columns of mindless figures.

Tuesday afternoon, Elisa watched Mrs. Carrots help some of the children bake Christmas cookies. Outside, on the now very empty riverside, Robert roughhoused with some of the boys. They were all staying here through the New Year and had no idea that she would be gone in two days. That was her secret – hers and Robert's. London was only a few hours journey, but Elisa felt like it was the other side of the world. Desperate to keep the secret, she and Robert promised not to speak privately. Feeling frightfully nervous, she was drawn to a spinet piano in the common room. She found a book of carols, and played through every song without stopping. Some of the children sang along. Their piping voices helped her forget her worries.

*

Robert knew Elisa was terrified. His heart ached, but there was nothing he could do to comfort her. Amelia Carrots saw everything that went on in the house. He was sure she suspected something, and expected her to pounce at any moment, demanding to know their scheme. Far back in his mind, he wondered if the canny woman was hoping Elisa had an escape plan. The entire school had seen him painting Elisa's portrait. They had spent hours alone together, behind those very public glass walls. Now, they were acting like strangers. As the hours went by, and Mrs. Carrots ignored them both, he felt sure she was protecting herself. If she didn't ask outright, she needn't lie later on. She could honestly say that she knew nothing about their plan.

Wednesday morning, Robert took the boys out to play rugby. Elisa sneaked back to Nicholas House. She carried her clothes to the art studio, and packed them into boxes identical to ones containing Robert's paintings.

Thursday morning, while Elisa gave Sarah a piano lesson, Robert went to the studio, sealed and addressed Elisa's boxes, then marked them with a small red X. Later that day, freighters collected his paintings for shipment to the Gildstein Gallery in London. Her clothing went with them.

The night before Elisa was to leave for London, she and Robert stood at the kitchen sink, helping with the washing up. The maid-of-all-work bent over a wash tub, scouring a roasting pan. Mrs. Carrots was in the common room, surrounded by children making paper ornaments. One of the older boys read aloud. A saucepan clanged into the sink and Elisa cried out, startling everyone.

Robert forced a laugh. "Careful there, butterfingers. We don't want to break anything." Holding his forced smile, he turned around. Mrs. Carrots stared back. She was not smiling. When he turned back to the sink, tears were streaming down Elisa's face. He turned the water on full, and whispered, "Pull yourself together."

In the other room, the boy continued reading.

Elisa swallowed hard, trying desperately to control her sobs. "I'm frightened."

Robert was seething. "So am I. Did you talk to the milkman?"

"He'll come for me at 5:30." Her tears kept flowing.

"Good. Just find the theatre. Michael will take care of you." A child wailed and Robert turned to see a small boy with a bleeding finger. Before Mrs. Carrots could lead him into the kitchen, Robert whispered, "Run upstairs and stay there 'til morning. I'll say you were taken ill. Go!"

After everyone had gone to bed, Robert stayed in the warm drawing room. Too nervous to sit still, he triple checked the list of paintings he had sent to London, wrote an inane letter to his mother, and tried to read a book. Once the fire was out, he went into the master's suite, cursing himself.

You've done some bloody stupid things in your time, but this is over the top. You'll end up in jail, you stupid sod, and for what? So a pretty girl can have an adventure and probably end up married to the filthy bugger she's run away from in the first place?

Shivering, he pulled off his clothes, threw on a night shirt, wrapped a robe around it, and stirred the dying coals. *And what have you gotten out of it? A damn good painting, and what else? Not a sodding thing. Bloody little virgin. She's a little witch. That's what she is. I wish I'd never met her.*

His door flew open and quietly shut. He turned and gasped. "Elly!" She was inside the room, her back against the door. Like Ophelia, her eyes were red from crying, her hair hung long, and wild. Delicate bare feet and ankles showed under a loose night dress. She was irresistible. "Oh, my darling!" He opened his arms and she flew into them.

174

He kissed her passionately, lowering her onto the rug. They rolled, hugging, squeezing, starving for each other's mouths. He pushed her nightdress up to her knees and she lay back, opening her legs. Startled by her compliance, he stroked the smooth flesh inside her thighs. His fingers reached further to her soft curly red hairs and soft folds of her skin. She writhed with pleasure.

He kissed her throat, and her lips, whispering, "Oh my darling girl, do you want this?"

"Oh yes, please!" She arched her back.

"Are you sure?"

"Yes!"

"Really?"

"Yes!"

Expecting to feel Robert's gentle fingers, Elisa was startled to feel his stiff organ push inside her. It was exciting. Lucy Ann's parents liked to do this so it must be all right. Robert pushed harder. Suddenly, it hurt.

Robert was thrilled until her face contorted in pain. He pulled away, gasping. "I'm sorry. But, you said you wanted it."

"I did want it." She sat up, breathing hard. "I thought I wanted it. I didn't know it would be like that." A blood stain spread on her nightdress. "I thought it would feel nice, like when you to touched me in the grotto."

"Shall I do that now? Please let me…" He reached for her but she pulled away. "I'm sorry I hurt you, darling, but always hurts the first time. The next time, it will-"

"We may never have a 'next time.' After tonight, we may never see each other again." Tears streamed down her cheeks.

Her words felt like a knife in his heart.

"I need to wash out this blood." In a flash, she was out the door, up the stairs and out of sight.

Frantic to go after her, he stayed where he was. If he was caught with her now, he would surely go to prison. He closed the door and sank to the floor. His heart pounded. His night shirt was soaked with sweat. Her virgin blood covered his hem and he hurried to wash it clean. When his wits cleared he checked the time. It was 2:30. The milk man was coming at 5:30. He could not her go without seeing her again.

He started to write a note, then threw it in the fire. Anything in writing could condemn him. He pulled on his trousers, wrapped himself in a blanket, and took a chair to the back door. An unbearably icy draft blew through the door jam, so he moved his chair a few feet out of the way. Determined to stay awake, he counted the ticks of the clock, sang songs, and recited poems. Finally, the verses failed. His head fell to one side. He was deep asleep.

*

Upstairs, Elisa furiously washed the blood from her nightdress. I'll go to London and get a job, any job. I don't need a man to protect me. I'll be my own woman. I'll be fine.

Tears threatened, but she willed them away. They're looking for a beautiful girl. I won't be beautiful if I keep crying. I won't get any beauty sleep tonight, but I can sleep on the train.

At 4:30, she was dressed, waiting for the milk man. At 5:00, clutching her small traveling bag, she crept down the stairs, through the kitchen, to the back door. She stopped short when she saw Robert asleep. He looked vulnerable, almost like a child. Tempted to wake him up, she steeled herself, quietly opened the door, and tiptoed past.

*

A rattling sound woke Robert from a deep sleep. His neck ached and he had to remind himself why he was in a chair by the back door. Suddenly recognizing the sound to be a horse and cart, he raced outside. The milk wagon looked small in the distance. It turned a corner, disappearing from view. He ran frantically, chasing after the cart. Freezing air seared his lungs. He could never catch up. She was gone. Feeling more desolate than he had ever felt in his life, he stared down the empty road, collapsed onto the cold ground, and cried.

End of Book 1

About the Author

Christina Britton Conroy is a classically trained singer and actor who has toured the globe singing operas, operettas, and musicals, as well as being a Certified Music Therapist and Licensed Creative Arts Therapist. She has published several books, and *Not From the Stars* is the first in the four-book *His Majesty's Theatre* series.

If you enjoyed *Not from the Stars* check out Endeavour Press's other books here: Endeavour Press - the UK's leading independent publisher of digital books.

For weekly updates on our free and discounted eBooks sign up to our newsletter.

Follow us on Twitter and Goodreads

Made in the USA
Columbia, SC
01 February 2023

11414522R00107